BEYOND THE RANGES

Dennis W.C. Wong

CLEVERCLOCK
PRESS

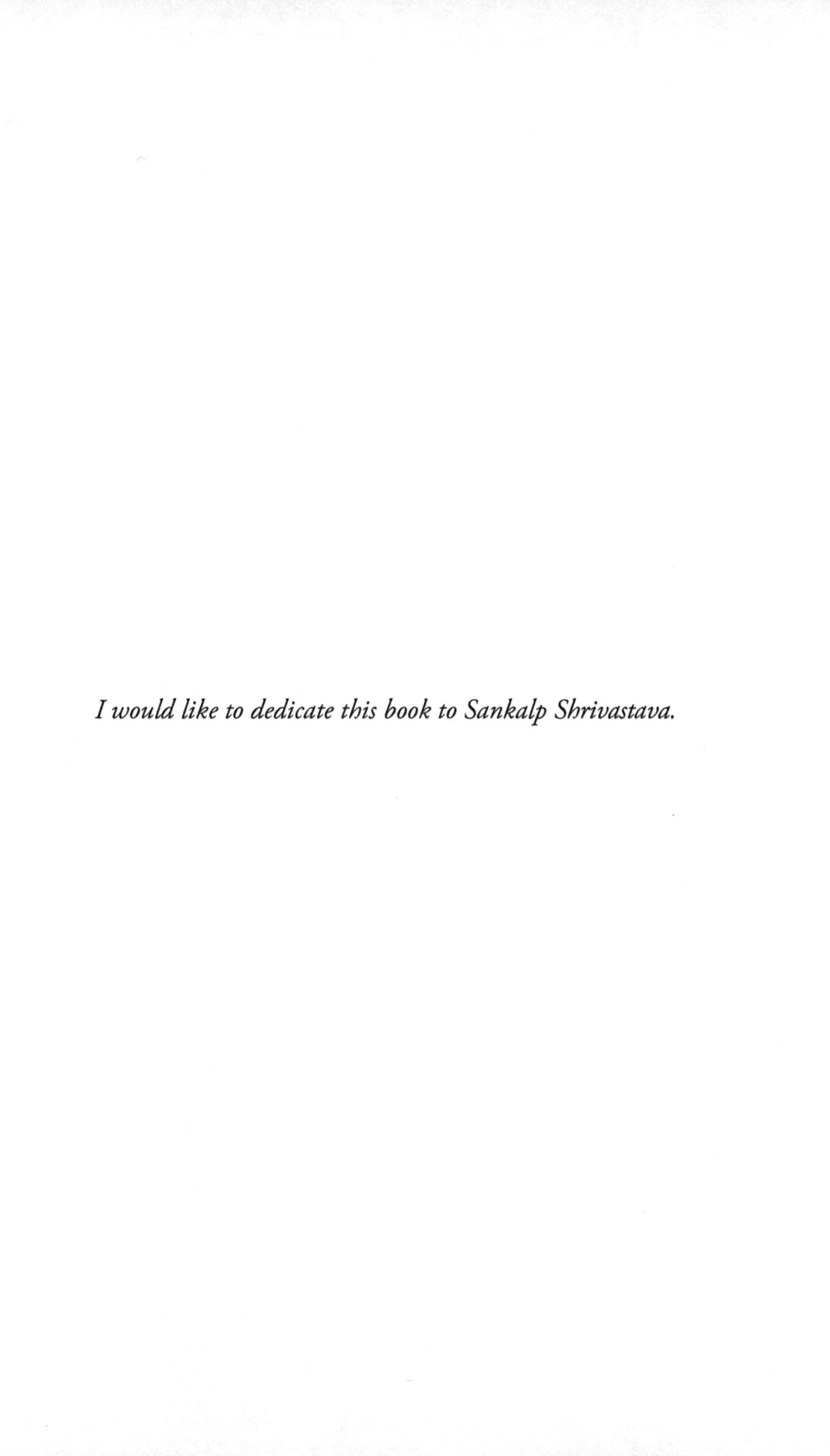

I would like to dedicate this book to Sankalp Shrivastava.

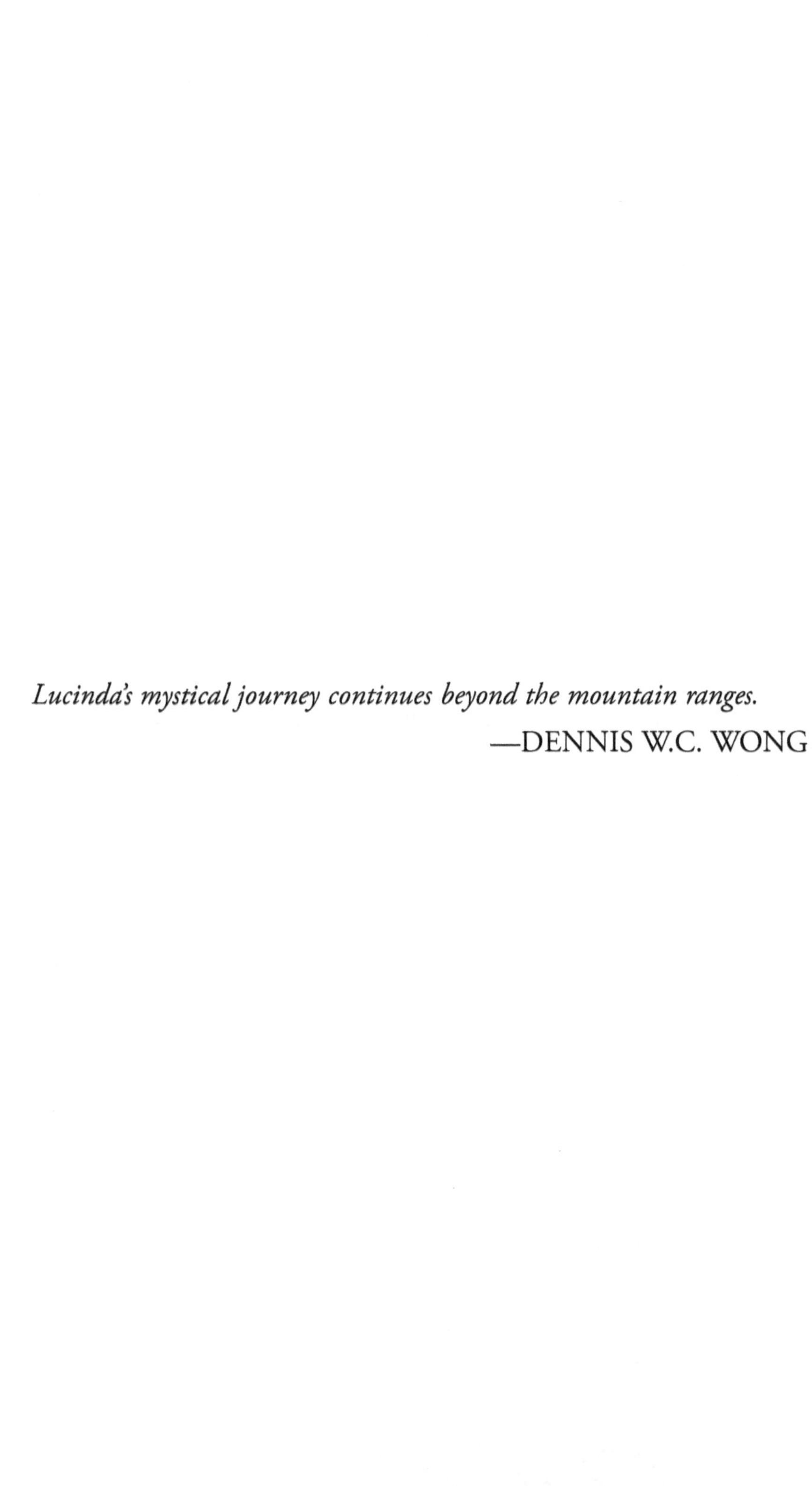

Lucinda's mystical journey continues beyond the mountain ranges.

—DENNIS W.C. WONG

Contents

INTRODUCTION

Mysteries, mysticism, the supernatural - all became a mosaic of Lucinda's world. She never thought she was going to hear from them again.

Lucinda had gone back to her father's house hoping to see her parent's spirit, but only to realize once more that she wouldn't be able to see them. Instead, she could only hear them.

◆ ◆ ◆

IT HURTS THAT
I CAN ONLY HEAR YOU

Chapter-1

It hurts that I can only hear you, but I can't see you. I can't even see Dad. Where are you?" Lucinda screamed with tears dripping down her eyes.

"I understand how you feel, Lucinda. But unfortunately, you can never see us again. We were given the privilege of communicating with you. So, let's be content with our voices only, okay, baby girl? The voice assured.

"Dad's, that's you?" Lucinda said as tears continued to stream down her cheeks.

"Yes, that's me. Let's be grateful, Lucinda, very grateful that you can still hear us." The voice replied.

"I am, Dad, I am," Lucinda said as she wiped the tears from her eyes.

"Time to go home," Lucinda said as she patted the horse, which slowly started moving and edged towards the mountaintop. Once home, she took the horse to the stable and went straight inside the house. Maya and Greg were sitting on the wooden chairs, chatting and laughing.

"You're back," Maya remarked.

"Happy birthday, beloved grandchild," Greg said, smiling.

"Happy birthday, my granddaughter. Where have you been?" Maya asked.

"I went to celebrate my 17th birthday at my parents' house and to see if I could see them again. It could have been the biggest gift in my entire life, but the situation remains the same. It's frustrating." Lucinda replied and walked inside, wanting to be alone at the moment.

"What is she saying? Did you promise her anything?" Maya asked.

"No. I do not know what Lucinda was saying. I will talk to her later." Greg replied.

After several minutes, Greg left Maya in the sitting room and walked into Lucinda's room.

"Can I come in?" Greg said, holding the door open.

"Grandpa, you are already in. Please come in." Lucinda replied.

"What's the problem, baby girl? You're not happy, and today is your birthday. You left early in the morning, and you came back with a frown on your face. To make matters worse, you said something that neither your grandmother nor I understood." Greg replied.

"How will you feel when you get a piece of cake only to discover that half has already been gone? How will you react to that?" Lucinda asked.

"I will feel bad, but I will be grateful for even getting holding of any cake at all," Greg replied.

"Why are you also talking about being grateful? I'm grateful. I am, but my parents should have just made the whole thing complete." Lucinda replied.

"Excuse me, young lady. Anna and Phil died seven years ago. So, what exactly are you talking about that your parents are making? What complete?" Greg replied.

"You don't understand, do you?" Lucinda asked.

"Of course, I don't understand. That's why I'm asking to know what you mean," Greg replied.

"Grandpa, my parents spoke to me actually."

"Lucinda, don't tell me you have finally lost it?" Greg asked.

"Grandpa!" Lucinda shouted.

"Lucinda, what's your problem?" Greg asked.

"I'm not crazy. You just asked me a question, which I was about to reply to, but you just cut me off. You know what? You can never understand, so don't worry about me. I'm fine. Never mind." Lucinda replied.

"Okay, since you said so. I have something to tell you." Greg said and waited for a split second before continuing, "We are moving."

"Moving? Moving to where? This place is nice. So, why do we have to leave here?" Lucinda asked, sitting up properly.

"The world is changing, and we have to move alongside it. We have to move to the city. I wanted to tell you that yesterday but I had to wait to tell you today because today is your birthday. I thought you would be happy about it." So, Greg said as a matter of fact.

"Happy about what? I'm not happy. Why do we have to move? I want to remain here." Lucinda replied.

"Growth is constant just as change is. You don't have to remain stagnant," Greg replied, patting her on the back.

"Growth, change. All these you mentioned can still be experienced here. I like it here so much. There are so many memories to hold on to. You can't expect me to wake up and tell me we're moving. No, that will not happen. Listen to me, Grandpa."

"No, you listen, young lady; we're moving, and that's final," Greg said.

"Perfect, and my parents and secondly by you completely ruin my birthday. So, you and Grandma can go. I can stay here, all alone. I want to be here; this is my roots. This place is my identity, and for me to leave here, I don't think it will happen." Lucinda replied.

Greg became intrigued the more. "How did your late parents ruin your birthday, Lucinda? What are you not telling me? You know you need to talk, young lady." Greg said, looking at Lucinda, expecting answers.

"You can't understand, so what's the need explaining? You just asked me a few minutes ago if I had lost it. I'm not crazy, Grandpa." Lucinda shouted as she stood up and ran out of her room.

Greg stood up and walked out, only to meet Maya close to the door.

"What happened? Why did she run off like that?" Maya asked.

"It's going to be hard convincing Lucinda to move with us to the city. She doesn't want to go. She wants to stay here and keeps talking about her late parents. Maybe if we move to the city, Lucinda might accept the reality that her parents are gone for good, that they are not coming back. My grandchild is going crazy. She is losing it, and the least I can do now is to take her far away from here." Greg replied as she left Maya and walked to the backyard.

Maya sighed as she went to the balcony where Lucinda sat down, holding her chin in contemplation, but with visible traces of tears on her cheeks. Maya sat close to her as she wiped the tears off her face.

"Why will a princess be crying even on her birthday?" Maya asked, throwing her right hand around Lucinda's shoulders.

"Grandpa wants us to leave for the city. Are you aware of this?" Lucinda asked?

"Yes, I am. Although there are many memories here," Maya replied it isn't harmful to start afresh.

I don't want to; I want to be here." Lucinda replied.

"Listen, baby girl. We need to leave. We are going with the horses if that's what you're scared of, but we need to leave. We need to see what the outside world looks like. Don't worry; if you don't like it, we will come back here, okay? It's a promise I'm making to you right now." Maya replied.

"Are you sure?" Lucinda asked.

"I swear on my very existence," Maya said.

Lucinda hugged her as they both smiled at each other.

"So, let's get back inside and have dinner. Today is your birthday, and I prepared your favorite for dinner. I bet you're going to like it." Maya said.

"Thank you so much, Granny," Lucinda said as the both of them stood up and walked inside.

When they finished their dinner, Lucinda took the plates to the kitchen to wash. Then she retired to her bedroom and walked toward the window, opening it and looking outside and up to the sky to behold the sky covered with beautiful twinkling stars.

"Who would ever think that I would leave here so soon. This move to the city hurts so much." Lucinda muttered under her breath.

"Maybe you should just listen to them and leave with them. You can still come back here when things change in the city." It was the voice of her mom.

"Can you hear me, Mom?" Lucinda asked.

"Everything, Lucinda. I'm just like the wind, but I'm always around you. I only speak when it's necessary. Listen to your grandparents, and when it's time, you must return to the mountaintop so you don't put the lives of the innocent at stake." The voice replied.

"Lives of the innocent at stake? What do you mean by that? Does it seem you know so much about the future? Please tell me." Lucinda replied.

"Never mind. When you get to the city, and when it's time for you to leave, just leave with your grandparents. That's the only thing we know for now." The voice replied.

"My roots are here; my identity, everything. It hurts that even you and Dad are asking me to go. I can't do it." Lucinda replied, cleaning off the tears in her eyes.

"Even if you don't want you to go, we need you to go so you can protect your grandparents. But Lucinda, my dear, this life is way deeper than you think. I already said this before, when the time comes for you to leave, leave with your grandparents. Because what we see, you might not be able to handle it." The voice replied.

"If we get to the city, will I ever hear from you both again?" Lucinda asked.

"Of course you will. We will be with you every minute of the day. That shouldn't get you worried." The voice replied.

"Alright then. Mom and Dad, goodnight. I need to sleep. Talk to you both tomorrow." Lucinda said as she shut her windows and went straight to her bed. Her mom's words kept ringing in her mind - "When it's time for you to leave, leave so you don't put the lives of the innocent at stake," what does that mean? What is going to happen to us if we get to the city?

If something terrible is going to happen, why don't they ask me to stay back? Why do they want me to go? Why?" Lucinda kept thinking about so many things before she closed her eyes and drifted off to sleep.

The following morning, Lucinda woke up in high spirits and did her chores. She took time to bathe the horses, and when she finished, she went inside to have her bath.

Shortly after, Maya called her to come out for her breakfast, but she insisted on eating in her room. When she was through, she told her grandparents she was going to her parents' house to say goodbye before they leave for the city tomorrow."

"Won't you take the horses with you?" Maya asked.

"No, I'm okay. It can be a long journey, but I can do it. I did it when I was ten, remember?" Lucinda said.

"Lucinda!" Greg called.

"Yes, Grandpa!" Lucinda answered.

"I'm sorry about yesterday. Please be careful and make sure you come back before night falls. Don't worry, Maya will help you and arrange your clothes while you are away, okay?" Greg said.

"Thanks, Grandpa," Lucinda said and smiled as she walked out of the house.

It was already noon when Lucinda finally got to her parents' house. She stood momentarily at the entrance with mixed feelings and then sighed loudly before opening the door and walking inside. As soon as Lucinda entered, she looked around and let out a sigh again.

Finally, after staying for a few minutes without uttering a word, she walked out and went to her parents' bedroom.

"I'm leaving. I just came to bid the house my last farewell because I don't know when I'm coming back, but I will surely come back someday." Lucinda said as she walked out and went straight to the parlor, where her parents' portrait laid on the center table. She picked it up as she left the house.

She then went straight to the river. She sat down on the riverbank when she got there and brought out the picture as she stared at it.

"I know you can see me, Mom. I wish you were here to hold me and see how much I have grown and how much I look like you and Dad." Lucinda started sobbing silently." This is the only thing I have in remembrance of you as I go to the city. I will never forget your face as long as I have this picture." Lucinda said as she stood up and started her journey back to the mountaintop.

◆　◆　◆

LUCINDA WITH GRANDPARENTS GOT TO THE CITY IN DELAY

Chapter-2

Lucinda with Grandparents got to the city in delay, but they could get to the house. No sooner had they settled in, Lucinda threw a question at them.

"You seemed to know much about the city. Where are we?" Lucinda asked.

"I've been here twice. After your fifteenth birthday, I had no choice but to decide to move to the city with you so you could forget what happened. I could buy this with the little savings we have, and here we are now." Greg replied.

"Grandma, did you know about this?" Lucinda asked.

"Sure, I did, but I felt it wasn't the right time to tell you," Maya replied.

"Interesting. Where is my room? I need to sleep." Lucinda replied as Maya took her to her bedroom.

"This is your room, and it's bigger than the room you had on the mountaintop. I made sure I put everything you like." Maya said.

"Thank you," Lucinda replied as she sat down and pulled off her sandals. She then lay on the bed, and in no time, she was off to sleep.

In the morning, when Lucinda woke, she saw an owl perched on her window. When she stood up to go close to the window, the owl flew off.

"An owl on my window this early morning? What could that mean? Is this ominous?" Lucinda thought as she opened her windows.

"The environment looks beautiful and serene, as you will soon find out. We even have a garden in the backyard where we can get to plant whatever we want." Greg said as he walked into the room.

"Good morning, Grandpa. Yes, I just looked around through my window. It sure looks enticing. You know I'm in love with nature, just like you and Grandma." Lucinda said, smiling.

"Good morning, my little angel. Your Grandma asked me to give you this. You had nothing to eat throughout yesterday, so she woke you very early to prepare this for you." Greg said, dropping a plate of food on Lucinda's bed.

"Wow! Thanks. It was so thoughtful of her as always." Lucinda said, grinning.

"So, did you want to look around through the window, or something else happen?" Greg was about to ask when Lucinda interrupted him.

"I woke up to see something off about here. I know you will say it's because I don't like the city, but I can feel it. It feels like I'm sensing something already," Lucinda replied.

"Don't worry. Once you get used to this place, I promise you will like here." Greg replied as he walked out of the room.

Lucinda cast a glance at the food on her bed before walking outside. She made straight for the garden at the back of the house. On getting there, she found a concrete bench there, and she sat down to have a look around and savor the morning's freshness.

"The beauty of nature is right here in my presence," Lucinda muttered as she sat down, closing her eyes to inhale the sweet smell oozing from the many flowers in the garden.

Immediately she opened her eyes and heard a noise, but she wasn't sure from where, which made her get up directly and race to her room. On closing her door, she sat on the edge of the bed.

"I'm 100% percent sure I heard a rumbling of voice or voices. It felt like someone crying out for help, asking me to go and never come back. Who was that? What could this mean? Something is odd about this place; either the city or this very house." Lucinda had fleeting thoughts as she kept looking about wildly. She went through the backdoor so her grandparents wouldn't notice she was leaving the house, and in no time, she was out on the street.

She met people going about doing routine affairs, with everyone minding their business. They were smiling, but suddenly she noticed the same smiling faces now wailing, asking for help. On looking around, she noticed she was the only one seeing those people.

"What is happening to me?" Lucinda thought aloud. "Why do I see all these?" She felt within her.

She couldn't contain it anymore as she turned and went back home. Her grandparents were surprised when they heard a knock and went to check who it was just to discover it was Lucinda.

"How come? How did you leave the house with no one knowing?" Maya asked.

"I went through the back door. I needed some fresh air and to see the city for myself." Lucinda replied.

"Lucinda, why is your face this way? Hope everything is okay?" Greg asked.

"I told you coming to this place will be a bad idea. I just can't take it anymore." Lucinda replied, leaning on the wall.

"What happened?" Maya and Greg asked almost at the same time, surprised.

"Asking what happened isn't the issue. The issue here is that you both will never believe me. So, let's just go back home." Lucinda replied.

"This place is home too," Greg replied, a little impatient.

"Maybe for you, but not for me. I just wish you can see and hear them. Maybe only then will you understand." Lucinda said and walked out before turning back.

"Please, none of you should come to my room. I just don't want to talk about anything." Lucinda said as she left, sobbing.

"But what's wrong? Why are you crying?" Maya asked.

"Just this once, Granny, just this once, please. I want to be alone for now, please, please." Lucinda said, and walked out on them.

"What's wrong with her?" Maya asked.

"We both saw what happened. I'm equally confused as well. I just don't know what to say." Greg replied.

"Maybe we should talk to her," Maya suggested.

"She made it clear she wants to be alone for now. Maya, listen, I know you still see Lucinda as that little girl that ran from the village to the mountaintop to tell us about her parent's demise, but I want to remind you that Lucinda is growing.

She is seventeen. Her parents might have died when Lucinda was ten, but to date, Lucinda hasn't accepted that they are gone for good. She is hurting, and as long as she remains on that mountaintop, she would never accept the reality.

So, we are not going back to the mountaintop. I know it's going to take time for her to get used to this place, but at the same time, I need her to heal from that pain. The only place she is going to heal is here, not there, where all those memories are still fresh in her mind." Greg replied.

"I didn't realize she was going to be like this, even after many years," Maya replied.

"What do you expect, when her parents were the only friends that she ever had?" Greg replied.

When Lucinda got to her room, she locked the door from inside. She felt she needed to understand what was happening around her, just her first day in the city.

"Why do I see all these? Why do I have to be the only one seeing them? Why has life been a terror, even after taking my parents away from me?" Lucinda said, crying.

"Life isn't torturing you, Lucinda. We raised a strong girl who didn't give up all these years after our departure. So, what makes you think you can give up now?" The voice of her mom asked.

"Then why do I see those horrible things?" Lucinda asked.

"What did you see?" the voice asked.

"So, you can't see them too?" Lucinda asked, surprised.

"No, we can't. But maybe if you tell us, we might help." The voice replied.

"When I went out today, I got to meet people going about their normal business, smiling. Suddenly, it felt like I saw them crying, asking me to leave, and that I had brought perpetual suffering to them. They were bleeding while calling out for help and looking around me. I became sure I was the only one seeing things." Lucinda replied.

"Lucinda, my child, those are just signs of what will happen when you don't leave on the required date. When that time comes, we will ask you to go back to the mountaintop, for what is coming is greater than you, and I doubt if you can take it." The voice replied.

"What is coming, Mom? Tell me." Lucinda demanded.

"We don't know for sure, but it won't be good." The voice replied. After considering their words, Lucinda took out her box, took out the magic Seashell and rubbed her hands on it.

"Can you at least show me what's going to happen? Tell me what the future holds for me. I'm getting scared already. At least I should know." Lucinda said, crying.

"Even the Seashell won't tell you what's going to happen in the future. Do you know why the future lies in your hand, Lucinda?" The voice replied.

"I don't know. I need someone to tell me what's going to happen." Lucinda replied, crying as she dropped the Seashell on the bed.

Lucinda lay on her bed curled up, disturbed.

She needed help and knew she couldn't ask her grandparents for help because they would think she had gone insane. She knew she was in this alone.

****

Lucinda found herself on the streets only to meet drops of blood everywhere. She couldn't fathom what was happening.

Finally, she yelled out, but everything was as silent as a graveyard.

She ran back home and called out to her grandparents, but she was greeted back with silence. The whole place was deserted.

"What's happening?" Lucinda asked, bemused.

"So, you don't know what's happening?" A voice asked as Lucinda turned to see a little girl standing at the door. It wasn't just any little girl; it was her replica from when she was just ten. Lucinda recoiled, thoughts racing through her mind.

"Where did you come from? Where did everyone go? Who are you?" Lucinda asked.

"I don't know. The entire city is deserted. My name is Lucinda." The little girl replied.

"That's my name, and you look exactly like me when I was ten," Lucinda observed.

"That's because I'm you. I'm from your past, Lucinda." The girl little replied.

"What do you mean?" Lucinda asked.

"You're letting fear consume the better part of you, and it isn't good. We're strong; we're queens who have been destined to rule immortals in the world beyond, but the question is, why are you giving up when we haven't even started the race? You're already backing down. Mom and Dad asked you to leave; will you leave?" The little girl asked.

"I have to. They said something bigger was coming and that I can't take it. I'm worried about my grandparents; I don't want any evil to befall them." Lucinda replied.

"If you left, generations of unborn would suffer for it, but that's not all. Grandpa and Grandma will get wet when the rain falls, and I'm sure you don't want it to happen.

But, no matter how far you run, no matter how long you shield yourself from realizing the truth, it will come knocking at the door someday. You must answer and guess what, it will be late by then.

Mom and Dad want you to leave because they feel you can't tame what's coming in front of you, but if you can't take it, kill it, Lucinda." The little girl said as she turned to leave.

"Where are you going? Please don't go." Lucinda pleaded.

"I'm going so you can return to the present world. This place isn't for you. I only came to convey a message. Goodbye." The little girl said as she vanished from sight."

Lucinda started sobbing as she heard a knock from a distance.

On opening, her eyes still crying. Lucinda realized she had been dreaming, with tears dripping down her cheeks.

"Lucinda, open the door, please," Maya shouted.

"I'll be out in a few minutes. So don't worry about me; I'll be fine." Lucinda said.

Her grandmother's knock brought her back to reality. What just happened? She thought. How could her ten-year-old self convey a message to her? How is that even possible? So, she felt as she stood up and walked towards the door to unlock it.

"You have been in there all day. Come and have dinner." Maya said as soon as Lucinda opened the door.

"Are you saying this is evening already?" Lucinda asked, totally lost.

"What's the time, Lucinda? Are you sure you're alright? You know you can always talk to me." Maya reassured.

"Don't worry, I'm fine. I'll be out soon." Lucinda replied as she watched her grandmother walk to the sitting room.

Lucinda lay on the bed as she kept recalling what happened in her dream, shivering at her recollections. Goose pimples appeared and disappeared on her body as she continues to think about those things. Myself as a ten-year- old, talking to me? How is that even possible?

Suddenly, she left the room and went to the sitting room to join her grandparents at the table for dinner. Soon after, her grandparents started throwing questions at her, but she responded with one-word answers, assuring them she was okay. She knew they wouldn't believe anything she would tell them, so she felt there was no need to say to them.

After they finished their dinner, Lucinda cleared the table and took the dishes to the kitchen to wash them off. Once she finished up, she quickly retired to her bedroom.

Just as she closed her eyes to sleep, she heard the voice. "Queen of the immortals."

Lucinda flipped her eyes open, but she saw no one. She closed her eyes tightly as she drifted off to sleep.

****

Lucinda had gotten to a pathway where a ray of light almost blinded her eyes; she could barely see what was on the other side. But she tried crossing over, it felt like something held her, preventing her from moving from where she was.

"You invited us, yet your body is filled with so much fear; why is that so?" a voice said.

"I didn't invite anyone. Who are you? It isn't my mom's voice, neither is it my dad's own, so who are you?" Lucinda yelled.

"Your subject." The voice replied.

"My subject? I don't know what is happening, and neither do I know what you're referring to. I've never felt responsible for anyone else apart from my dead parents and my grandparents. So, who are they? Or has my life suddenly become something else that I do not know? Have I unknowingly become something else, having some sort of subject?

Two people are so important to me in my life, but they left so early. They are the ones that I would love for them to come back if I ever had the chance.

And if there were anything I could do to bring them back to life, I'd readily do that. I don't know you, and I don't want you to become my subject. Just stay where you are and allow me to live my life the way it pleases me. And talking about fear, you can't blame me.

You can't blame a seventeen-year-old girl because, for the past seven years of my life, I've been trying to heal from the death hurled against me by taking my parents away at a time most unexpected.

Please don't add to my sorrows, whoever you are!" Lucinda replied, almost shouting.

"You are the queen. You invited your subject over here. You asked me to come. Your presence in this city woke me up, yet you can't summon the courage to talk to your subject." The voice persisted.

"Ha! What! I am not your queen, and I don't want to be. Take back your crown. I don't want to be a queen of any kingdom that I don't know. Just leave me alone." Lucinda yelled.

"How can I take the crown that was given to you even before my very own existence? And it's not a kingdom, but a world different from the world of humans. You will forever remain queen of the immortals.

When I finally get here, please welcome us, or we might cause perpetual pain and agony to the surrounding people. Please do not allow fear beclouding your inherent boldness. I can still remember that girl who ran from the village to the mountaintop just to tell her grandparents about the demise of her parents.

The same courageous girl who ran without fear, not minding the dangers on the road, that's the girl we know, not this new Lucinda who has been consumed by fear." The voice replied.

"How do you know my name? Who are you, and what do you want?" Lucinda asked, more disturbed than afraid.

"It's forbidden for a subject not to know the name of their queen. My name is Anya. I want nothing." The voice replied.

"What journey are you talking about?" Lucinda asked.

"The journey that lies in front of you, of course. The path is full of thorns.

The path is slippery. It is dark. We don't know what lies ahead, but you will need my help when the time comes because that's your fate, but before then, I need to make my presence known in your world where you live. Goodbye, Lucinda." The voice said.

"What is happening to me? Why am I going through these? I never wanted to come to this city. Ever since I arrived here two nights ago, everything around me had been ominous; not for once have I had any reason to smile. What kind of stupid fate do I have?

Why do I have to go through all these alone? Why wouldn't death had taken me too when it took my parents?

I wouldn't have been going through so much pain. You all don't love me or even care about me because if you did, somehow my parents would have been here; you would have spared me. It hurts. I want to be alone, free from all this drama. I'm going to mourn my parents for as long as possible.

They deserve every bit, and they are worth it. Do you know why? Simple: Because of them, there will be no Lucinda." Lucinda said as she sat down and wept, and as she was sobbing, the light that had almost blinded her became dim, but no one was there anymore.

"Lucinda!" Her mom's voice sounded.

"Mom, that's you. Where are you?" Lucinda asked, looking around, but to her dismay and disappointment, she was alone. She shivered as she opened up her eyes only to discover she had been dreaming all this while.

She stood up as she walked closer to the window and opened up to let in rays of the twinkling stars.

"What's bothering you, baby girl?" The mom's voice continued as she opened the window.

"Dad, Mom, I'm scared. I just wish to leave this city. I'm tired of everything that is happening around me. I just wish to be free. I'm afraid of what the future portends." Lucinda replied.

"Fear, that has always been the problem right from day one. Can you at least trust yourself? The mom's voice replied.

"Mom, you have always encouraged me whenever I want to do things, but the fear aspect, I think I took that from you and yes, Mom.

You once mentioned that whatever I see and doubted that I could handle it. What's that? Maybe you can explain better now." Lucinda asked.

"You ask too many questions, Lucinda. The journey ahead of you is way deeper than what we think, and it's connected to so many things. We don't know what's going to happen, but we doubt that our baby here can handle it." The voice replied.

"I'm seventeen, Mom; I'm no longer a baby." Lucinda reminded her parents.

"Even if your mom doubts you can win what lies ahead of you, I somehow know my girl. The dad's voice replied.

"Thanks, Dad, but you two do not understand. My life has turned into something else. I wish for these to end. What differs from what Grandpa and Grandma see. I've told you what happened yesterday.

I stepped out of this house when I saw people calling out to me and asking me to leave. They were in pain, and that they were hurt.

Later I saw blood where everywhere and people asking me to return to wherever I came. But, of course, I'm talking about what I saw with my two eyes. And just now, someone I did not even see or had ever met called me, "Queen of the immortals."

Every human being born of a woman is bound to die someday, so where do these immortals live, and why can't I see them? Why am I a queen in a world where I know nothing?

Why was I born into this world if they knew I was going to suffer? I'm tired! I'm tired, and I wish to go back to my old life there on the mountaintop where no one will call me a queen, where I won't be seeing things differently from all others around me.

You both might think I'm crazy, but the truth is I'm not. Apart from yours, I keep hearing voices in dreams and real life. The last one I spoke with said the name is Anya. I don't know what Anya looks like, but the voice sounded feminine.

She said if she comes and I don't welcome her, she will bring pain to people around me, and guess what, I will be held accountable for it. Am I making sense to you both, or do you think your daughter is crazy?" Questions, questions unanswered, or perhaps unanswerable." Lucinda concluded.

"No, you're not crazy, but have you told your grandpa and grandma about these experiences of yours?" Her dad's voice asked.

"Not yet, Dad. Besides, they will think I'm crazy," Lucinda replied.

"Yes, they will because you're different from them. You're not who you think you are. I don't even know the power you possess because only the one with a strong power can hear people from the other world.

And about the people you see on the streets, that's just fear trying to get hold of you. Fear makes you think that something worse will happen if you stayed here for as long as you want.

Your mom wants you to leave when the time comes, but I want you to stay. I want you to fight this. I have always known you to be a strong girl, and I know the future is bright.

Surely the path will be filled with thorns and thistles, but I know you will scale through. Don't let what you're seeing deprive you of finding out who you are.

I have known you to be a normal child ever since you were born, but today, the child I gave birth to is a different person all along. You can do this, Lucinda, yes you can. Just let go of all those negative thoughts in your head." The voice replied.

"Thanks, Dad, but how come Mom isn't saying anything anymore," Lucinda asked.

"She will talk to you tomorrow, but remember, don't let fear win." The voice replied. Soon after, Lucinda heard a knock on her door, and she walked towards the door to open it.

"Grandpa." Lucinda softly called as she went to a chair that was close to her window.

"Why did you leave the windows open, and why are you awake by this time of the night?" Greg asked.

"Oh, I had a dream, so I woke up, and I opened the windows. I needed to see the sky. How about you? Why are you also awake?" Lucinda asked.

"I wanted to get water to drink, and I thought I should check up on you when I heard you call Mom and Dad. Who were you talking to?" Greg asked.

"Oh, I was talking to my parents," Lucinda replied.

Greg contemplated on Lucinda's words. To him, it was apparent that she was depressed. He just didn't know what to do to his grandchild anymore.

"Why are you looking at me that way?" Lucinda asked.

"You're still hurt over your parents' death. You're not over it yet, but I'm sure that soon you'll get over it," Greg said.

"You need the truth, Grandpa?" Lucinda asked.

"Yes, tell me the truth. I want to help. Tell me what the problem is, you can't keep living like this forever. You need to let go." Greg pleaded.

"I'm hurt, yes. I'm angry, yes. Life took my most priceless possession when I had just a decade with them. They might be dead, but they are around. We might not see them, but they live among us. I just want to mourn them for as long as I can.

If I mourned them for two or three decades, they are worth it because there wouldn't be any Lucinda if there were no Anna and Phil. I miss them, and I can't let go, no matter how hard I try. That's the truth. I appreciate everything, Grandpa, but healing is a journey, and I'm not ready yet to embark on it." Lucinda replied.

"I miss that little girl that you were, and I would do anything to bring that smile on her face again," Greg replied.

"I miss that little girl I was too. I miss her." Lucinda replied.

"Then why did you let pain change you? Why, Lucinda?" Greg asked.

"Fate, fate caused it all. Just maybe, death should have spared my parents." Lucinda replied.

"Lucinda, please, we need you back. Heal for us. That pain is hurting us too." Greg replied.

"When I'm ready, I will heal, but before then, I wish to ask you a question," Lucinda said.

"Sure, why not?" Greg enthused.

"Was there any mystery surrounding my birth?" Lucinda asked. "Why did you ask?" Greg asked.

"I just want to know. Is there?" Lucinda asked, looking at Greg in anticipation.

Hmmm. My dear, you're exceptional. On the night of a full moon, your mom, Anna, made a wish. She said, "I want my daughter to be a queen even though we're poor. Let her be a queen even in this world and in the world beyond."

That was her wish that night. So, when I walked up to her, I told her she wanted you to be a queen here on earth and in the world of immortals.

She said yes, she knows she wants to give the entire world to you. And when she gave birth to you, you had this birthmark on your back, the shape of a full moon with stars surrounding it.

You can barely see it because it's on your back. When your mom saw that, she laughed and said even the stars granted her wish. Aside from that, there is nothing else." Greg said.

"I'm a daughter of the moon and the stars? But is there anything like the world of the immortals?" Lucinda asked.

"World of the immortals? That I don't know of, but that birthmark made your mom believe the stars and moon granted her wish, and yes, the mark means you're the daughter of the moon and the stars." Greg replied.

"And the seashell?" Lucinda asked.

"It was said to be magical, but little is known about that because I don't know what it does," Greg replied.

"Alright, thanks, Grandpa. I will just go back to sleep now." Lucinda replied.

"Alright, goodnight," Greg said as he walked out of the room.

Lucinda locked the door as she lay on the bed, immediately soliloquizing. "This explains it all. She was crowned even before she was born, and that was my mother's wish." Lucinda closed her eyes as she drifted off to sleep.

As soon she woke up in the morning, she stripped herself naked and turned her back to the mirror. She saw the birthmark and wondered how come she never saw it before. Then she put her clothes back on.

"Lucinda, leave." Mom's voice came in as soon as she was through wearing her clothing.

"Leave to where Mom?" Lucinda asked.

"You need to leave this city before the night of the full moon. Please, you need to go, as you may not survive what is coming." The voice persisted.

"Why are you getting me scared? Just explain to me why I must leave." Lucinda asked, a little irritated.

"There is nothing to explain; just leave before the night of the full moon; that's it." The voice ordered.

"Don't let fear win" were the words from her father, and she remembered them vividly. So, ignoring her mom's words, she zipped her button and walked out of the room.

ON THE DAY
OF THE FULL MOON

Chapter-3

On the day of the full moon, Lucinda kept pacing around her room, thinking of the best possible way to alert her grandparents of a looming danger. She needed to talk to her grandparents so they could leave the city that night.

Lucinda wanted them to be safe, for she had already sensed that what was coming was ominous, and she didn't think she would be that brave to face it.

After pacing up and down for some time, Lucinda left her room and went straight to the sitting room. Luckily her grandparents were sitting down their chit-chatting.

"We need to leave today before nightfall." Lucinda simply announced as soon she entered and sat down on the sofa opposite her grandparents. Greg and Maya were bemused at her, moping at her with stirring emotions.

"Leave to where? We don't understand. I mean, why should we leave so suddenly?" Maya was the first to find her voice.

"We need to leave here. We need to go back to the mountaintop, please." Lucinda pleaded.

"Why? You have not answered Maya's question. Lucinda, what's wrong? Are you okay?" Greg asked, still moping at her.

Lucinda considered their questions in her mind before blurting out: "If we don't leave, we might all die. We might get consumed by what's coming. Just trust me." Lucinda pleaded more.

"Lucinda, please don't tell me you're going insane. What's happening to you?" Maya asked.

"I'm okay, everyone; we just need to leave before nightfall," Lucinda shouted.

"Why, why do we need to leave? Talk to us, child. Stop being uptight. Allow us to help you." Greg said.

"Please, we need to leave. I'm begging you both. Listen to me; I have never made this request before. Let's just leave." Lucinda.

"Why Lucinda? Who asked you to talk to us to leave because I'm sure you didn't wake up this morning to blab this silly idea of yours? Maya asked.

"A voice from beyond." Lucinda blurted out, unable to hold herself anymore.

"What do you mean?" Greg asked.

"I just answered your question. I said a voice from beyond asked me to tell you we need to leave today before nightfall. Mom asked us to leave." Lucinda replied.

"I will not sit down here and listen to you utter all these words from your mouth. After the incident with the horses, it seems you have lost your mind completely. What is happening to my grandchild?

Understand that your parents are dead; they were my children too. Anna, your mother, was my child, but I have accepted their demise in good fate. It's been years, Lucinda, seven good years.

You're yet to accept the fact that they're dead. Your grandmother and I brought you here hoping that you would heal and forget all about them, but it seems not working. Now answer me, Lucinda, when will you heal? When will you accept that Anna and Phil are gone for good?" Greg asked, a bit irritated. Lucinda didn't waste time before answering Greg.

"You spent quality time with your daughter before she got married, and I spent only a decade with her. How do you think I could recover from that pain, like you, how Grandpa? No matter how hard I try to explain, you both will never understand. Besides, this is beyond healing and still bleeding. You keep misjudging me; you keep misreading the situation. I have already accepted the fate that this journey is mine alone to embark on. I lost my parents at the tender age of ten; already accepted by me, but I'm not ready to lose you both now, and that's why I'm asking you to please let's go back to the mountaintop where it's much safer." Lucinda replied, wiping the tears already gathering, off her eyes.

"You might delude yourself, Lucinda, but we won't share in your delusion. I have watched you all these years, and I know you've yet to accept the demise of your parents. That's what is affecting your thought processes." Greg said.

"That's what you think, but they are not gone yet. They are immortals by my side, speaking to me, just as we are now talking, hearing my every word, and I hear their words. That's the fact you have refused to accept!" Lucinda shouted.

"Lucinda!" Maya shouted.

"You both want the truth? Maybe I will tell you, though I know it's useless. My parents aren't gone. I can hear them. I can hear them loud and clear, and it was Mom's instruction that I should take you out of here because what's coming is evil, and I might not handle it.

You both might not hear Anna and Phil speak but trust me, they mean well for us. The same way you both want me to heal, that's what they want too; that's why they talk to me every day. All these years, I have received nothing but love and care from you both. You both had been my parents.

I can't compare the love you showered on me with anything, and I'm grateful, but the truth remains that I miss my parents. They left when I needed them most in this journey called life.

They left when I least expected it. I slept with my parents' corpse in the same house. My parents died most painfully. They didn't deserve to die the way they did.

The only way nature compensated me was by giving me the ability to hear them, though they are in the world beyond.

So please, I'm not insane; I'm not crazy; stop thinking that way. I'm only fighting to make sure we all stay alive. Please let's leave." Lucinda pleaded.

"The answer is no, Lucinda," Greg replied.

Lucinda stood up and threw one look at them before running back to her room and shutting the door.

"What's happening? Why is this happening? Why can't they make this easier for all of us? Why?" Lucinda asked as she sobbed silently, throwing herself on her bed.

"Is fate playing on my grandparents, making them adamant in their decision to stay back, so I could stay back too and fight?

How can I fight this when I don't even know what it is? Why will generations of unborn suffer for this? Why should I be placed in the center of all this? Why must it be me? Why, why me?" Lucinda was muttering as she continued to toss herself on her bed.

"Because you're a queen destined to rule immortals in the world beyond." The voice said, which made Lucinda turn in the direction it came from, but she saw no one.

"That wasn't my parents' voice. So, who could that be?" Lucinda asked as she stood up and walked closer to the window.

"Don't let fear consume you; if you can't take it, kill it, Lucinda." The voice said.

"And that's all? Who is talking to me? Why can't you just show yourself?" Lucinda asked, casting furtive glances around.

"The dream, yes, the dream. Now I remembered; she said these exact words to me, but how can I kill? How can I have my hands stained with blood? No, I can't. I don't know what is coming, but I'm not killing it." Lucinda said, sighing.

"Then tame it. You'll be glad you did because, in the future, you will need its help." The voice replied.

"I just need to take a nap. Then, maybe when I wake up, I'll be able to think of how to keep Grandpa and Grandma safe from these," Lucinda muttered as she went back to her bed before shortly drifting off to sleep.

****

"Maybe we should listen to her," Maya said.

"And head back to the mountaintop because of an illusion? That will not happen.

I love Lucinda so much, and I would stop at nothing to make sure she is healed from this pain. I don't care how many more years it will take to put up with this nonsense, but I'm willing to wait.

And if I die today, I would be annoyed with myself. Do you know why? Because I would feel I didn't try hard enough for my grandchild to heal from the pain caused by her own parents' death.

I will stop at nothing to bring back the old Lucinda. This new Lucinda isn't the girl that spent her holiday with me years back then, full of life and laughter.

This new Lucinda is uptight, sad, and she is in pain. I just want her to be happy again." Greg replied.

"I know, only that I simply don't like the way things are going. I want nothing to happen to Lucinda; or us yet." Maya said.

"Nothing will happen to her or us," Greg assured.

****

Shortly after a brief sleep, Lucinda woke up and instantly bent over under her bed to pick up the seashell. She took it out and laid her hands on it.

"I'm worried; I'm worried over the life of my grandparents. You need to protect them. I wouldn't want the rain coming to wet them. Please protect them for me. I know they would never leave. I have tried talking to them. I have explained, but the ultimate answer was no. So, please protect them for me.

Shield them from what is coming. I can sense it; it's huge. I would never forgive myself if anything happened to them." Lucinda as her eyes became wet. She held herself back from crying.

That night after Lucinda finished with her dinner in her room, she went back to her grandparents' room; and saw them fast asleep. She then walked back to her room, but looking outside, she saw the moon was fading its color to red.

"Hmmm. The Blood Moon! It's almost midnight." Lucinda muttered under her breath as she went close to her window.

Shortly after, it was midnight; and Lucinda started feeling goosebumps all over her body. She just didn't know what was happening.

Lucinda wanted to leave the house and walk on the street, but somehow, she could restrain the power urging her to go. Soon after, she started seeing blood on her palm.

"What is happening?" Lucinda asked when she saw she was bleeding from her hands. She had no injury on her body previously.

Nevertheless, Lucinda was frightened, and as soon as the drop of her blood touched the floor, she instinctively glanced at the moon again to see it had changed to a full blood moon, shimmering in its incandescence.

The howling sound that followed frightened Lucinda to her marrows that she quickly shut her windows and recoiled back to her bed.

"They are here. They are here for you, and they would never leave till they see you. The earth needed your blood for the full moon to turn red; that's why I asked you to leave. I think you can fight what's in front of you." Her mom's voice said.

"But Mom, I can't do this; I don't want to fight anything that I don't even know," Lucinda said.

"You have to. I believe you can do this because if you don't, the wails of people from this city will deafen your ears." The voice replied.

"Mom, what do you mean?" Lucinda asked.

"Blood shall be spilled. That road filled with people will be silent like a graveyard. This city will turn into a graveyard, and you wouldn't want that to happen.

You conquered your fear when you choose to stay, following your grandparents' refusal to leave.

I believe you can tame what's in front. It's in your hands; it's your fate. Goodnight, child." The voice said.

"Why do I have this fate? Why am I destined to go through so much in life? Why is my life this way?

The only thing I wanted was to grow up with my parents right beside me as a child.

But I grew up experiencing their death and, after that, hearing only their voices. Now I'm being asked to protect a city I barely know.

It's just been only four months of staying here. So why do I have to go through so much? Why? Why?" Lucinda asked as tears trickled down her cheeks.

"Don't let fear win, Lucinda. Why are you getting yourself so worked up when you know no journey has ever been that easy for you?

The problems are just there to make you better and strengthen you than you were before, Lucinda. You have always been a strong girl.

Don't tell me you're giving up now because of the problem that is here. What happened to that Lucinda that I know before I died?" It was her dad's voice.

"That Lucinda is still here, Dad. That Lucinda didn't change. I'm only scared that people might get hurt because of me." Lucinda asked.

"Oh really? Is that what you think? People won't get hurt because of you. Even if they get hurt, then try to calm the situation. You have always been a good leader." The voice replied.

"Yes, Lucinda can do this," Lucinda said as she walked to her bed and lay down. She closed her eyes, and before she knew it, she was fast asleep.

When she woke up in the morning, the first thing she checked was her palm, but there was nothing to show that she bled the night before. Lucinda stood up and walked out of the room to the sitting room. She opened the door, walked out, and saw if anything happened in the night.

Strolling on the road, Lucinda could see drops of blood as people kept murmuring about it. Looking at them, it was apparent they were terrified of what happened and not knowing who the next victim would be. They spoke in hushed tones.

Lucinda turned, and she strolled back home, troubled. She met her grandparents discussing in the sitting room.

"Where did you go?" Greg asked.

"I just went out. It seems lives were lost after what happened last night. There were drops of blood on the road." Lucinda replied.

"That's bad. That is so bad." Maya replied.

"More will still happen; more lives will still be lost. We could have averted this if we had left the city yesterday, but no, you both thought I was crazy. I wonder what pain the family will go through right now." Lucinda replied, taking a seat.

"What happened last night has got nothing to do with us. So, what are you saying?" Greg asked.

"The incident of last night has everything to do with me. I told you bringing me to this city was a terrible suggestion." Lucinda replied as she stood up and walked into her room.

"Mom, if you can hear me, I want to ask you something," Lucinda called as soon as she entered her room.

"What you saw this morning was the main reason I asked you to leave. Your dad wanted you to stay and asked you not to let fear win, but I was scared. So, staying here is a terrible suggestion." She sounded solemn and worried.

"About my birthmark: what's the story behind it?" Lucinda asked.

"It seems I made a wish, and it came to pass. When I was still carrying you in my womb, I had made a wish on the night of the full moon, and I had asked that you should be a queen.

We had little, and we are mere commoners, but I wanted to give you the world, and when I had you, I saw the birthmark, and I knew my wish came through.

So, you're my queen, and I believe one day the world will bow before your feet." The voice replied.

"Oh, now I understand. You just collaborated what Grandpa told me about the mark; and why they kept calling me their queen." Lucinda said.

"What do you mean?" The voice asked.

"Don't worry; I will figure all these out by myself. I believe I can." Lucinda replied.

"What are you going to do?" Lucinda asked.

"Never mind, and about the birthmark, why didn't you tell me all this while? I never saw it until Grandpa and I had a discussion, and he told me about it, and when I checked the next morning in the mirror, that was when I saw it. Why did you keep quiet about it for ten years, Mom? And even now, you still didn't say a word about it until I asked. Why do I feel there is more surrounding my birth? What else do I need to know?" Lucinda asked.

"I never told you because I didn't see it as anything, and the birthmark was on your back making it difficult for you to see." The voice replied.

"Is there anything else I need to know about my birth? Tell me more. Did anything strange happen after you gave birth to me?" Lucinda asked with bated anticipation.

"That night, I heard howls of wolves. I guess your dad was fast asleep, so he didn't hear the howls." The voice replied.

"Hmmm." Lucinda grunted lightly before thinking silently: "I might not be normal, like every other person. But I think I'm different. I'm the daughter of the moon and stars. I possess powers I don't even know. Mom asked I guess she received more than what she asked for."

"Why are you silent?" The voice asked.

"Never mind, Mom. I'm just trying to wrap my head on something." Lucinda replied.

"You have nothing to worry about. We are here for you. Though you can't see us, it's an enormous privilege that you can hear us. I love you so much, Lucinda, and even in death, I would still give the entire world to you. You're still my baby, my best friend, and my only child. You can never walk on any path alone. Your father and I will always be around to make this journey easier for you." The voice replied.

"Thanks, Mom," Lucinda replied.

"But you have to send them back, or else; the entire city might suffer for this." The voice replied.

"How do I send them back? I don't know how to know to do that." Lucinda replied.

"Even myself, I don't know how to, but I know with time, you will figure out how to do that. I trust you, Lucinda. I know you can win this." The voice replied.

"Thanks, Mom," Lucinda said, smiling.

"Lucinda!" Maya called as she knocked on the door.

Lucinda stood up and walked to the door of her grandmother.

Maya walked in as she sat down on Lucinda's bed, tapped the bed, and instructed Lucinda to sit down.

"Is there anything we need to know?" Maya asked.

"No, nothing, but maybe if you tell me exactly what you mean, I could be able to answer the question," Lucinda replied.

"You spoke about your dead parents being able to communicate with you. So, what happened yesterday's night had a link with you. Can you let me in those?" Maya asked.

"Hope I'm not interrupting," Greg said as he walked inside.

"So, can you answer the question?" Maya said after glancing at Greg. "Well, everything I said out there is the truth and nothing but the truth.

What happened last night? It's all my fault. Just maybe you both should have listened to me.

We should have left peacefully and still come back later. Mom asked that I take you both out of here, your daughter Anna, not even her husband, Phil.

She saw what's in front, and she asked that I leave though Dad asked that I stay back and conquer whatever it is. They are coming for me.

It's just a matter of time, and they shall get me." Lucinda replied.

"Maybe we can still go back since we're going to return afterward," Maya replied.

"No. We're not going anywhere. Lucinda, what's wrong with you?" Greg asked.

"Everything is wrong with me. Maybe you should have stopped Mom when she made that wish. Maybe if you had cautioned her not to involve me with the world of the immortals, I would have been free from everything happening since their death, but you kept quiet.

You keep thinking it's all about my parents' death, that I'm suffering a psychological breakdown because of that. How long could that be? Seven years? No Grandpa. I'm hale and sound, very aware of my environment, of everything happening, mostly what neither you nor Grandma can see or hear.

It's not a psychological breakdown. I'm not losing my mind! The trigger for these is traceable to Mom's wish seventeen years ago.

As it stands, wish has ruined everything. My life, my happiness, and it's so unfortunate I will have to live the rest of my life with that."

Lucinda yelled as she stood up from her bed and made for the door, leaving them with their mouth agape.

"Where are you going because I still don't understand everything you have said here? How do you expect us to believe you're talking to your parents for crying out loud, Granddaughter? They are gone. They are dead!" Greg said, exasperated.

Lucinda turned and, looking at her grandparents, and she said: "That's the only problem here. No matter what, you can never believe it.

Please stop asking me what the problem is since you have always refused to believe me.

Stop asking me. It's your problem, not mine, whether you believe me. I have never lied to any of you before, yet you find it hard to believe when you both ask me questions. Hence, my problem is my problem.

I only can find the solution. I do not need your help, as you can see. If you cannot believe me, how can you find a solution for me? Impossible!" Lucinda yelled with tears in her eyes and walked out.

"She is hurt, but why is she talking about the wish Anna made years ago? I'm yet to understand how it ruined her life." Maya asked.

"Perhaps, the moon wants her daughter back," Greg replied as he stood up and left the room. At the moment, things weren't making sense to him, but somehow, he was determined he would get the truth from Lucinda. He knew she was going through something.

But unfortunately, that problem was way too much for her to handle, from the look of things.

As Lucinda left her grandparents, she went straight for the stable at the back of the house. As she opened it and walked inside, she held the white house and pulled her outside. Then, she mounted her and whispered something into the horse's ear as they galloped off.

She was going back to her parent's house in the village. She felt she just needed time to think. She knew before she would return, it would already be late in the evening.

After two hours, Lucinda got to her parent's village and strolled down to the river. On getting there, she came down from the horse and sat on the river bank. Then, after a few minutes of quietness, she started throwing pebbles into the river.

Soon after, a voice sounded from her behind: "Hello." Lucinda turned to see a pretty young lady standing behind her.

"Do you mind if I join you?" The lady asked.

"Sure."

"I'm Mia, and you're?" The lady asked.

"Lucinda."

"I've been observing you from a distance as soon you got here. It seems you're bothered about something. Do you mind sharing it with me?" Mia asked.

Lucinda sighed, took a glance at Mia. She picked a pebble and threw it into the river before opening it up to Mia. "My heart is heavy, and right now, the wish my mother made years ago is coming back at me.

It seems the problems are way too much, and I'm afraid that I may not handle them. I just feel I can't do it, that I can't win the battle that lies ahead." Lucinda replied.

"Is that all?"

"Sure; that's all."

"Well, as for now, there are no battles, but there will be battles in the few months to come. Besides, what you see as a problem isn't a problem at all; it's just a task that needs to be done." Mia replied.

"What do you mean?" Lucinda turned to have a good look at her as she asked.

"Yea, you're scared about the howls of the wolves you heard at night and the drops of blood you saw this morning. They came for you, but they are not here to kill you or hurt you.

They will hurt more people if you don't welcome them. She already told you that. So, if you don't welcome her, she will cause more pain and agony to people around you; and about the seashell, it can't protect your grandparents for a long time.

Time is going quickly, Lucinda, and if you don't tame that which has come for you into this world, more lives will still be lost. As for your grandparents, don't convince them anymore as they will never believe you, but the truth is they love you so much more than life itself and will give the entire world to you.

You're different; you're the daughter of the moon. You're a queen who was crowned even before you came into this life." Mia said.

Lucinda stood up as she took a step back from Mia.

"Who are you? How did you know she said she was coming, and she was going to cause pain to everyone around me, and how do you know so much about me?" Lucinda asked.

"Anya, that's her name. I guess you have forgotten. When they told you they were coming, they weren't joking." Mia replied.

"They? Who are they?"

"Anya is three in one, an amalgam of the sort, both a deadly beast and a wonderful soul. So, you choose which side of her you want." Mia replied.

"Who are you, and how did you know all this?" Lucinda asked.

"You are finding it hard to solve the puzzle in front of you. Now I have helped you solve it. I guess you know the right thing to do now. Tame the beast or send it back." Mia replied.

"Tame which beast? How can I tame what I don't know?" Lucinda asked. "That's your puzzle to solve. No one has ever tamed Anya. Anya will kill more. Anya will render many useless, and she will come for your grandparents soon.

The magic of the seashell can't keep her away for long, and about the wish your mother made, it has always been in the prophecy.

But, Lucinda, you are the Chosen One; and Anya shouldn't be the problem now. The problem should be what you decide to do." Mia replied.

"But you said Anya is a deadly beast and..."

"A wonderful soul as well, depending on which side you want to see. But, trust me, what's in front is greater and deadlier." Mia replied.

"Who are you?" Lucinda asked again, clearly more afraid than angry.

"My name is Mia."

"I know, but who are you? How did you know all these?" Lucinda asked.

Mia laughed as she stood up and walked towards the river.

"Do I look beautiful?" Mia asked.

"Yes, sure, more than any human I have set my eyes on," Lucinda replied, genuinely enchanted by Mia's beauty.

"I'm the Goddess of this river, and I know more because I have existed for ages and ages. When you were drowning in this place years ago, I didn't want to kill you. I only wanted to show you a little about what your life is all about, but Phil came in time to save you.

The Moon and stars have waited for a long time, and they want their daughter to fix this as ordained." Mia replied as she walked into the river, and before Lucinda could say anything, she vanished before her sight.

"Thank You," Lucinda muttered as she hurriedly mounted her horse and galloped home, back to the city.

Once in the stable, Lucinda pecked the white horse together with the brown horse and smiled before leaving. It was already 6 pm when she got back home. Her grandpa sat on the sofa inside the sitting room, waiting for her to walk in. As soon as she walked in, he asked: "Lucinda, where did you go?

You took the horse, and you went off without even telling any of us. Where did you go to?" Greg asked.

"I went to my parents' house in the village. I just needed some time to think, and I guess I have found my answers." Lucinda replied, grinning.

"Sit down, let's talk," Greg asked as Lucinda sat close to him.

"I want to help, but I can't if you don't tell me what the problem is. I want to be part of it all." Greg pleaded.

"I just need to fix one more thing. Just give me some more time, and I promise I will tell you everything. Do you trust me?" Lucinda asked.

"I trust you, dear," Greg replied.

Lucinda stood up as she hugged her grandfather and whispered into his ears: "When the time is right, it will all make sense."

◆ ◆ ◆

LUCINDA WALKED INTO HER ROOM, AGITATED

Chapter-4

Lucinda walked into her room, agitated, as she kept pacing around. To her, it was apparent Mia knew so much about her. She considered going back to the river to see if she could meet her again, to find out how to end her dilemma. But she was in a quandary.

After pacing here and there, Lucinda had her bath. When she finished, she went back to the sitting room to have dinner with her grandparents. However, Lucinda wasn't feeling comfortable. She felt tense as she needed to find a permanent solution to her problem.

"Anya is already here, and she won't leave until I welcome her, but how will I welcome someone who has been described as a deadly beast by Mia? What if Anya feasts on me immediately when she sees me?" She muttered.

"What's wrong, child." The voice of her dad asked.

As soon as Lucinda heard the voice, she sat up and moved closer to the window. Then, she unlocked the window.

"What's the problem?" Her dad asked again.

"Anya is the problem. She will never leave," Lucinda replied.

"And who is Anya?"

Just then, the howls of the wolves sounded. It was midnight.

"The voice you heard is that of Anya. Dad, Anya stays and won't leave till I welcome her." Lucinda replied.

"But that's three; I can hear three voices." The dad replied.

"Anya is three in one, a deadly beast and also a goodly beast. I don't want to meet her." Lucinda replied.

"You said something about welcoming Anya. How do you intend to do that, child? I can see you're already searching for answers which means you haven't given room to fear. I'm happy about that."

"Yes, I'm searching for answers. Unfortunately, I haven't found the exact thing I'm looking for.

I need to welcome Anya, whom my presence brought into this world, and even if she must leave, I must welcome her first.

I can't see myself doing that, and if Anya stays for long without seeing me. More souls will be lost. She will continue to kill many. I was told that even the magic seashell couldn't protect my grandparents for a long time, which means Anya will come knocking someday." Lucinda replied.

"Will you let that happen?" Her dad asked.

"No, I can't let that happen. I can't let Anya hurt my grandparents. If anything happened to them, life would lose its meaning to me. I need them here; I can't be left alone." Lucinda replied.

"Then you have to welcome Anya. Even if you don't know-how now, I know soon you will come up with an answer to that. I have always believed in you. I won't even stop soon," he said.

"Thanks, Dad. Thanks for your words of encouragement. Tell Mom that somehow, I will end all this and let her know Anya won't hurt her parents or me. I will find a means soon to send her back." Lucinda said.

"Alright, my child," said he.

Lucinda walked back to her bed as she lay down and stared at the ceiling. Before she knew it, she was already asleep.

The following morning Lucinda woke up early at 5 am when it was still dark. She stood up from her bed and walked out of her room, passing through the back door to the garden. She sat down on her favorite chair and started soliloquizing immediately.

"All my life, I never thought I was someone else other than a normal human being.

It's now clear to me that even my parents didn't know whom they gave birth to. My grandparents also think I'm just Lucinda, but now I know I'm something more.

Right now, I face the greatest task ever to tame a monster I have never seen with my eyes. How difficult can that be? My life changed in the twinkling of an eye. After so many years, it is now that I realize that I'm someone else."

"You're up too early. Why?" Her mom's voice pierced through her mutterings, but she was relaxed. She had grown accustomed to her parents' voices.

"How can I sleep knowing full well that many souls are in danger because of me? I wouldn't know how many just died last night. How do you want me to feel, Mom? I can't sleep. This very thing has robbed me of my sleep and peace of mind." Lucinda replied.

"Send them back." Her mom said.

"You already know it's not about sending them back, but how, and even if I can send them back, how do I welcome them first. If I don't welcome Anya, there is no way she is ever going to leave. So how do I face a deadly beast though she is also good? How? Tell me how Mom." Lucinda replied.

"I don't know, but I know you have to find out how or else more and more will lose their lives." She replied. Lucinda cupped her head in her hands as she was engrossed in thoughts.

Soon after, she stood and walked inside the house as she went to her bedroom. Lucinda was restless. She bent down, brought out a magic seashell from under her bed, and walked back to the garden.

Lucinda rubbed her hands on the seashell as her tears dropped on it. Her desire was for Anya to go back to the world she came from.

She was trying to see if anything could work out, as she didn't know how to go about anything concerning Anya.

"Don't bother because that wish isn't coming true; trust me." A voice said as Lucinda turned to see a beautiful lady sitting down close to her.

"How did you get here?" Lucinda asked.

"I was here already before you came. I'm everywhere." The lady replied.

"What's your name?" Lucinda asked.

"Berta, that's the name." She replied.

"And why did you say that my wish will not come through? Do you even know what I want to wish for?" Lucinda asked.

"You want Anya to go back to the world where she came, sure, but then even the seashell can't grant that. What you hold in your hand is one of the most priceless possessions of the Royals, but mind you, there are certain requests it can't grant." Berta replied.

"Then how do I make them go back? I want to send them back, more people are dying by the night, and more will still die if I don't send them back. Please, I need help." Lucinda replied.

"I can't answer that. I don't even have the answer to that question. No one knows how you can send Anya back. But you're the queen, so you should know how to tackle that." Berta replied.

"Why should everyone keep calling me queen? How can you all place a crown on the head of one who isn't interested in the crown? I want to be free like every other young girl out there.

I'm tired of been handed a task that I'm incompetent to handle. I'm tired, just tired. People are dying every night, yet I'm told that I should send Anya back for that to stop, and yet no one knows how to do that.

What's the meaning of all of this? I'm tired, and I need help." Lucinda blurted.

"You're asked to save people's lives now, and without yet doing anything, you're already tired. Well, if you continued this way, soon, you will be confronted with the option of choosing your parents or saving humanity." Berta replied.

"You are..."

"Joking? No Lucinda. I'm not joking. Maybe if Mia didn't tell you, I think I should let you know now. You're being asked to solve a minor puzzle, and you're finding it so hard to do.

Don't tell me you're letting fear get over you. I've not known the daughter of the moon and the stars to be a coward. No matter how hard you try to run away from this, this is your life.

Welcome Anya and save everybody of the impending doom from following.

Keep calm and watch the bloodshed happen to someone closer to you, and when I say that, I mean either your grandpa or your grandma." Berta said, standing up.

"How did you know Mia? How did you know she already met with me? Where are you from, and who are you?" Lucinda asked.

"Mia is the goddess of the river. I knew when and where she met you. She met you at her river where you almost got drowned years ago. I know because I'm everywhere." Berta replied.

"Who are you?" Lucinda asked.

"I'm a goddess, just like Mia, but I'm the goddess of the wind. Lucinda, the sooner you accept who you are, the better for everyone." Berta replied and turned to leave, but she stopped when Lucinda called out her name.

"You are leaving. Why isn't everyone helping me out with this puzzle? Is it so difficult to solve? I keep asking for help every day, but it seems everyone is ignorant of the solution. What is happening?" Lucinda asked as tears dripped down her eyes.

"That's because no one can solve the puzzle except you. Find answers to the puzzle, no matter how difficult it is.

The day you fully accept that you're not only a human, then that day, but you would also know why the birthmark is on your back and what it can do; that day too, you would know the powers you possess.

I hope you find answers to what you seek, but when it comes to helping. You can only help yourself." Berta replied and kept moving more profoundly, and right before Lucinda, Berta vanished into the wind.

"I'm everywhere, but you won't see me. Then, one day, we will all meet," Berta said as she remained invisible.

Lucinda shivered a bit, went into the sitting room, and sat on the sofa while still holding onto the seashell. Soon she was awoken with a tap on her shoulder. She opened her eyes to see her grandpa.

"Good morning, Grandpa." Lucinda greeted.

"Good morning, child. You're up so early; why are you with the seashell?" Greg asked.

"I'm only holding onto it as it somehow gives me strength whenever I feel weak," Lucinda answered.

"That's nice to hear. Hope you didn't sleep here the entire night?" Greg asked.

"Oh no, I didn't. I went out into the garden early, and I just came in and sat down here. I didn't know when I dozed off." Lucinda replied.

"How about Grandma? She asked.

"Oh, she is still sleeping," Greg replied.

"It seems you're still feeling sleepy. Wouldn't you rather go back to bed?" Greg added as Lucinda stood up and headed to her room.

She lay on the bed and drifted off to sleep.

"Grandpa, what are you doing here?" Lucinda asked.

She had found her grandpa sitting in a deserted place with blood oozing from his knee. On his knee was a bruise sustained because of his battle with a deadly beast.

What happened to you, Grandpa?" Lucinda asked as she placed her hands on the wounds trying to stop the bleeding, but on seeing it wasn't helping, she raced into the bush and came out a few minutes later with some leaves on her hands, rubbing the leaves on her two palms before squeezing out the liquid on the bruised knee.

Greg screamed in pain as Lucinda held on to him, and in no time, the knee stopped bleeding.

"Thank you so much, child," Greg said.

"What happened to you?" Lucinda asked again as she sat on the floor and stared deep into her grandpa's eye. Right in there in his eyes, she saw three fierce-looking wolves attacked her grandpa.

She saw how he tried to scare them away; and how the wolves didn't want to kill him. Instead, they just wanted to inflict pain on him.

"Wolves attacked you," Lucinda remarked.

"Yes, and I heard them talk. They will keep killing more and more souls till you welcome them. What connection do you have with them?" Greg asked.

"I don't have any connection with them, and I certainly don't know what they are talking about," Lucinda replied.

"Are you sure? Today it's me, and certainly tomorrow, it might be my wife, Maya. What are you hiding, Lucinda? Right now, I'm in pain because of you. You know they are here for you, yet you are reluctant to see them. Now answer me: how many more souls do you want to die before you can answer them, the very reason you came into this world?" Greg asked.

"How are you so certain they came for me?" Lucinda asked.

"Simple. They mentioned your name. They aren't just animals; they are enchanted. They speak in unison, and the message was clear: "Tell Lucinda to welcome us to the world she brought us into, else souls and souls will be lost." Greg replied.

I didn't ask them to come. I never summoned them to this world. I don't even know them. Now they're killing and hurting people close to me already.

How can I welcome them when I didn't bring them into this world? How do I even face something that I have never seen before?

I'm scared, Grandpa. I can't do anything. Because I want to put a stop to all this killing. I don't want to meet any beast; that's the only truth I know." Lucinda replied.

Greg stood up as she looked at Lucinda and said: "I want nothing to happen to my wife or you, child. I might have borne the pain they inflicted on me today, but I doubt if your grandma is going to bear the same pain.

They are not here to kill you. They want you to welcome them. You keep saying you didn't bring any of them to this world. I understand.

I believe you, no matter how hard you try to shy away from. You're the only one who can stop this killing. Yes, you are. Save humanity before you ruin it with your aloofness." Greg said as he began limping away.

"Where are you going, Grandpa? At least let me assist you." Lucinda pleaded.

"I don't need it, child. All I need is that you end this chaos before it begins. This chaos that you're avoiding will come knocking at your door someday. If you don't do the right thing before the time, it might also consume us all. You started this. Please send it away before you lose any of us." Greg said and walked away.

Lucinda covered her face with her hands as she sobbed quietly. What she was avoiding was already on her door. How can she end all this? How can she end this chaos?" Lucinda muttered amidst sobs.

"That's not true," said an aged voice.

Lucinda looked up to see an older woman sitting close to her.

"How did you get here, and who are you?" Lucinda asked.

"I don't have a name, but you can choose to give me any name you want. The man you saw isn't your grandfather, but it's just a clip of what's going to happen to him if you don't welcome Anya. You cannot summon Anya and refused to welcome her." The aged woman said.

"But I didn't summon her." Lucinda protested.

"You don't need to talk or even command for her to come to your world. Your presence here on earth summoned her. You need to do the right thing and welcome her before she unleashes terror to the entire humanity." The aged woman replied.

"But how do I welcome her? I have never seen Anya before. I heard she is a deadly beast as well. She is going to hurt me." Lucinda replied.

"You're so naïve, my child. Anya can never and will never hurt you. She can never hurt the daughter of the moon and the stars. She only needs you to do the right thing. The previous queen before you welcomed her, so why is it hard for you to do the same?" The aged woman asked.

"Okay. How do I welcome her? I want to put an end to this. And just like my grandpa, or rather his illusion, asked: "How many more souls do I want to die before I end the chaos that I have created?" Lucinda replied.

"Good, just before midnight, leave the house and go far away, just keep walking, when it struck midnight, wherever you are Anya will find you and you both will meet, but you must never cry in her presence, no matter how scared you are.

Anya must never see your tears. It is forbidden for the subject to see the queen in tears." The aged woman replied as she stretched forth her hand and asked Lucinda to place her hands on it.

"You're a young lady who had lost her parents seven years ago, and today you're still in pain. You're yet to heal. Your heart is heavy and filled with pain, sorrow, and sadness. You smile but beneath that smile lies a heart asking questions every day, demanding to know why her parents had to die so early.

The journey ahead isn't an easy one; more is still coming. A time will come when you will have to choose between your parents and saving humanity and your world as well. You're not just human.

You are two, and when I mean your world, I mean the world beyond because that's where you rightfully belong. The journey before you are going to be difficult, but please choose between saving humanity.

Goodbye, my child. You need to go. Maya and Greg will get worried if they don't see you soon." The aged woman said as she smiled and whistled gently before leaving.

Lucinda woke up as she rubbed her eyes, only to find out it was all a dream. The aged woman had sent her home with the whistle. She quietly stood up from her bed as she kept the seashell in the box.

She quickly had her bath as she wore her clothes and walked out of the room while her grandmother set the table for breakfast.

"You didn't wake me up to help you," Lucinda asked.

"You looked so beautiful in your sleep. At a time, you were even smiling, so I had to leave you. Call your grandpa." Maya requested.

Lucinda called her grandpa, who came out promptly, and they all sat down and ate breakfast. When Lucinda was finished, she went straight to the stable and bathed the horses as she left them outside to dry. She then cleaned up and dropped hay leaves for them.

"What bothers you, child? Your heart is heavy, and you don't look fine." Her dad voiced out.

"I have to welcome Anya. If I don't, more souls will be lost." Lucinda replied.

"Have you done that?" He asked.

"I have to meet with Anya, Dad. I'm terrified. I can't imagine standing and facing a deadly beast. It's so difficult, and if I don't do it, the killing continues, and someday it will come knocking at my door.

I wouldn't want Grandpa ever to witness what I saw in my dream. I just can't let that happen. Mom would say meeting up with Anya will be a bad idea, but she wouldn't be happy with me if anything happens to her parents.

The same way I was left under their care, that's the same way. They are now left under my care. I have to protect them at all cost." Lucinda replied.

"I wouldn't want you to get hurt, but I wouldn't want this to linger on. I believe Anya would never hurt you. Maybe you were chosen for a purpose. I know this task isn't easy, but I trust my Lucinda to get it done." He replied.

"Do you think I can get to face Anya?" Lucinda said, sighing.

"Who are you talking to?" Maya asked as she walked into the stable.

"I'm talking to…"

"She won't understand. So, no need to tell her. She will think you're going crazy." Her dad interrupted her.

"I'm not talking to anyone, Grandma," Lucinda replied.

"Okay, I will wait for you inside," Maya replied and walked out. Lucinda checked to see whether she was out of sight before saying: "How I wish they can hear you and Mom. Things would have been a lot easier." Lucinda said.

"But sadly, they can't. You're fortunate enough or should I say blessed with powers to hear us." Phil said.

I will have to succeed at all cost to end this, or I will die trying. I wouldn't want them to be hurt because of me." Lucinda replied.

"Alright, please try to smile for your mom and for me too." He mildly requested.

"I will, Dad," Lucinda said as she smiled. She took the horses inside and changed their water as she locked the stable and went back to the house.

No sooner had she entered her room than Maya walked into the room.

"Granny, you're here," Lucinda asked.

"Oh yes, now sit," Maya instructed.

"Oh, okay. Hope you're not about to give me lectures?" Lucinda asked, smiling.

"I heard you talking to someone when you said you couldn't believe you will have to talk to Anya. Who is Anya? I heard you say your mom won't be happy if anything happens to her parents, your grandpa, and me. So, tell me, Lucinda, who were you talking to?" Maya asked.

"I was not talking to anyone. Anya is the name of the beast that comes to the city every night," Lucinda replied.

"It has a name? The name sounds feminine, but how did you know all this?" Maya asked.

"Some things are better left unsaid, Grandma. I don't want Anya to hurt any of you because Mom would never be happy with me. The beast is still going around killing as many as she can. Even this house can't protect us from the beast. So, I have to do something else I might live to regret it for the rest of my previous life." Lucinda replied.

"How do you mean? You're getting me confused." Maya asked.

"Do you trust me, Grandma?" Lucinda asked.

"Of course, I trust you. I trust you so much, more than anything else in this world." Maya replied.

"Then believe me when I say, I will protect you both. Nothing, I mean nothing will ever happen to any of you." Lucinda replied.

Maya sighed as she stood up and left the room. There was no need to ask any more questions because she knew Lucinda wouldn't answer. The day went so well, and later that evening, they had their dinner. Lucinda didn't retire to bed immediately; she stayed back in the sitting room with them chatting. After some minutes, she excused herself as she went to the backdoor and unlocked it. Lucinda came back and sat with them with her face filled with smiles. She wanted to spend quality time with them because she was scared that she might not make it back alive after tonight.

◆　◆　◆

GOODNIGHT, GRANDPA; GOODNIGHT, GRANDMA

Chapter-5

"Goodnight, Grandpa; goodnight, Grandma," Lucinda said as she went straight to her bedroom. She didn't want her grandparents to know she was to go out that night.

Immediately it was few minutes before midnight when Lucinda was very sure her grandparents had gone to bed. She quietly tiptoed out of her room and out the backdoor. She had left the door unbolted so she could quickly leave the house with no one noticing.

Immediately she stepped her foot out of the house, and she walked gently on the street with the moon illuminating the pathway. She just needed to get to keep going, awaiting the midnight when she could meet Anya.

As she kept walking with nowhere in particular, as was instructed by the older woman, she suddenly started hearing sounds of howls of wolves, signaling it was midnight. And on hearing the sound, she lost her feet and tripped to the ground, and on getting up, she discovered she had bruised her big toe.

On getting up, with excruciating pain, she found she was face to face with her fears right in front of her–the beast, Anya, was right there before her.

Three wolves were right in front of her, but something was different about them. Their eyes were like that of the moon, illuminating like an incandescent globe. She watched as wolves brought their head down before her before speaking.

"It took forever for you to come for us when you are the same person who summoned us." The wolves spoke in unison.

"Summoned you? I never did. I never summoned you at all. I never asked you to come. You have done nothing but hurt innocent people who did nothing wrong to you. Why? Why would you do that?" Lucinda yelled, clearly angry instead of being frightened by the terror before her.

"Your presence on the night of the full moon invited us. Had you stayed away from here, we wouldn't have come?" The wolves replied.

"Well, I'm sorry that I was present, but right now I need you all to go, go back to where you came from. You have done more harm than good.

I just want to have my life back. I'm tired of seeing the people suffer, dying for what they are not aware of." Lucinda pleaded.

"Do you think it's that easy? You can't summon us and ask us to go back, just like that." The wolves replied.

"But I want you all to go back. Just tell me how then I will do it so you would go back to where you came back from. Anya, please, you have already caused so much pain to people I barely know, but although, I do not know them, they're dying because of me. I feel for them. I'm the reason for what has befallen them." Lucinda pleaded.

"All this wouldn't have happened. But you summoned me. You summoned Anya, and you didn't welcome Anya. You need to welcome Anya else Anya would cause perpetual pain and agony to people around you." The wolves replied.

"How is it possible that you animals are even talking and so strange that I can even understand you all?" Lucinda asked, though not entirely surprised.

"Maybe the sooner you realize that you're not just human, then all these will make sense to you. How did you think you could hear the voice of your parents? It's because you possess that supernatural power to hear voices from the great beyond." The wolves replied.

"What do you want, Anya? I'm ready to do it, so you can stop all these and then go back to your world." Lucinda replied.

"You can't send me back just like that, Lucinda. That's the only truth," Anya replied.

"I'm tired, Anya; I'm tired by all that is happening. I am. I just want to be like every other girl and live a happy life." Lucinda replied.

"But you are not like them; you're different. You're a queen crowned even before your birth. Your life was different, and no matter how you wish for it, your life is perfect." Anya replied.

"Goodbye, young queen. At least you have welcomed us." The wolves said in unison as Lucinda watched them vanish into a nearby bush.

Lucinda sat on the ground as her blood kept dripping into the soil.

"Do you mind if I check your leg?" The voice said as Lucinda looked up to see a woman squatting right in front of her.

"Who are you, and where did you come from?" Lucinda asked, a bit surprised to see she talked to someone she had never seen before, in the middle of the night.

"Don't worry. I'm not here to hurt you. I would never do that." The lady replied as she touched Lucinda's leg. She muttered some words, and the bleeding seized. No one would believe that she was bleeding from her big toe a few minutes ago.

"How did you do that, and who are you?" Lucinda asked.

"Call me Tara, the goddess of fire." The lady replied as she smiled.

"Mia, Berta, and now Tara," Lucinda thought inaudibly and then said, "Maybe you have solutions to the puzzle; you have the answers that I seek. How can I send Anya back? She has killed enough. She is a deadly beast, and staying here will endanger the lives of innocent people." Lucinda asked.

"The answers you seek for, I do not have them. You wish to send Anya back to the world beyond by all means, but I don't know. Like you know, Anya isn't just one; she is three in one, making her be one of the most powerful beings in existence. Anya is an enchanted wolf. I'm sorry, but the answers you seek for, I can't provide them." Tara replied.

"When am I seeing the earth Goddess as I'm yet to see her? Maybe she would have answers to my questions. Perhaps she could help me out of this mess." Lucinda replied.

"You're not in any mess. This is your fate. You already have been destined for this, even before your birth." Tara said as she stood up and headed for the surrounding bush.

"Don't tell me you're leaving. Why do you all keep coming when you can't give me answers to my questions? Why can't you all help me out? I'm tired, and I'm pleading for help. I only want to protect the lives of people around me. I know how I felt when I lost my parents seven years ago. I wonder what the family of those killed are going through right now. I just want to help them. I want everyone to be safe. Anya is the threat here, and she needs to leave." Lucinda pleaded.

"Hmmm. Well, then you have to know this. My dear, the people of this city murdered the previous queen decades ago before you were born.

Fate made you and your grandparents move back to this place, and for the lives killed, they are not innocent. Their hands had been stained with the blood of the queen before you.

Anya wants to wipe them off before coming for you. Anya doesn't believe in forgiveness; she believes in revenge. So, Anya plans to wipe the entire city and then come for your grandparents. She won't kill them, but she will hurt them.

How do you expect her to feel when this same city killed our previous queen? The pain is still fresh in Anya's heart. Now that you have met with her, I believe she won't shed any more blood.

Anya might be the deadliest of them all, but she has a sweet soul. Just too bad you met the other side of her first. And as for the earth goddess you think might have the answers to your questions, you're the fourth goddess Lucinda, the earth goddess," Tara replied.

"How do you mean? I don't understand." Lucinda replied, shivering a bit.

"When the time is right, it will all make sense to you," Tara replied and walked deeper into the bush.

Lucinda looked up to see that the moon was still shining brighter than ever. She fell to the ground and started crying, sobbing.

Nothing was making sense to her yet. With every episode that passed, she continued getting confused over the whole thing. How could she be the fourth goddess? She wondered in between her sobs.

"We came to you because you needed our help."

"You're one of us though you possess powers that are greater."

"We have answered the question we can, to the extent we know. It's now left for you to continue on this journey alone."

"We would return only when the time is right. We know you can win this." It was the combined voices of Berta, Mia, and Tara. Lucinda wished they could give her straightforward answers to questions welling inside her mind.

Soon after the voices sounded, Lucinda looked up to see a bright light showing from far away. She stood up as she advanced towards it, and slowly she walked into the light.

On entering the light, Lucinda saw herself in a different world altogether. She saw a girl who looked like her ran past her with tears in her eyes. Lucinda followed her closely as she watched the girl run into the hands of a mob.

"Please don't hurt me. I'm begging you. I did nothing. I'm innocent of all the crimes that I'm accused of. I didn't kill the king. He didn't die because of me." The little girl frantically pleaded.

She saw as the mob kept calling the little girl a liar, refusing to believe her. She saw as they started throwing various things at her. Finally, she saw them take her to a dungeon and locked her up as she cried bitterly.

"Why are you being tortured?" Lucinda asked, but she wasn't heard. Instead, she walked closer to the girl and touched her as she raised her chin.

"Why are they torturing you? What offense have you committed, and why is it that no one can see me?" Lucinda asked again.

"You're from the future; this is the past." The little girl answered.

Lucinda shivered on hearing that. She took a few steps backward and cast another glance at the girl before her.

"My name is Lucia, daughter of the moon and the stars. You're my incarnation. The people are torturing the people I would do anything for at any cost to protect and me." Lucia replied.

"Since the daughter of the moon and the stars, why didn't you have powers, powers to set yourself free from these people?" Lucinda replied.

"I do, but I have been rendered powerless to use it. If I should use my powers against them, then my parents will be killed. So, I rather die than live and watch them kill my parents." Lucia replied.

"What happened then? Why are they doing this to you?" Lucinda asked.

"I have never withheld my powers from doing good. I have used it to help and heal so many. Everyone loved and cherished me, and they termed me a blessing to their generation.

My people warned me that humans could never be trusted. I was pleased to keep my powers hidden, but I didn't. I felt we are all one family. The king had fallen ill, and as usual, I had gone to treat him.

He was perfectly okay when I left the chambers, but before I got to the gate, I was handcuffed, with claims that I had stabbed the king and I was trying to run away. I escaped, but somehow, they got my parents.

I didn't escape because I wanted to run away from them, but only so I could buy more time to see if I could get the killer.

The killer is from the world beyond. She will come to you but with a different face and name. For now, she is in hibernation. Fate has it that the one that owns the seashell can kill her forever.

In between, the people somehow got to find my hiding place, and now they got me, and here I am in this cage. I wanted to rescue my parents and leave this city together, but my plans didn't work. After all that I have done for this city, they still think that I'm capable of murder.

I have been betrayed and stabbed by them. You're wondering why Anya is killing souls, the souls you deemed innocent?

They aren't innocent after all; they came together and set me ablaze. They watched me burn to death despite my pleas and cries that I was innocent. I might have forgiven them, but Anya never forgets; Anya believes in revenge.

I'm happy that you have at least welcomed Anya, which means there would be no more bloodshed and that the city will be in peace again.

I have forgiven the souls in the city that killed me, but remember they were never innocent. They killed me.

They killed us. Keep your powers hidden from ordinary eyes. That is all that I want you to do." Lucia replied.

"I don't think I have any powers. My utmost concern now is how to put a stop to the bloodshed bedeviling the city people. The nightly cries and wails are becoming unbearable to me.

You said by my welcoming Anya that it would stop, but I'm afraid Anya will hurt my grandparents who live in the city. Anya might hurt them if she finds no one else to kill." Lucinda replied.

"When the time comes, you will know the powers you possess, but don't forget to keep it a secret. You're wondering why the people cannot hear you. Of course, they can't as you're not from this century.

You've been able to see what happened in the past because Tara made it known to you that the people whom you were fighting for, whom you thought was innocent, weren't really.

She is correct. Please don't repeat my mistake, your mistake indeed because I am you and you are me. Let your powers be your only secret that they do not know of." Lucia replied." But Lucia, I ha..."

"I don't have the answers to that question which you want to ask now. We're the same, you and me. You're just my incarnation, but soon, you will see the beauty of the great work you're called to do. So please go back to your world." Lucia replied.

Then before Lucinda's eyes, the gate to the dungeon was opened as some soldiers came and whisked Lucia away. Lucinda followed them as she watched them tie Lucia to a bunch of sticks.

Then, after pouring a liquid substance on her, they set her ablaze. She couldn't withstand Lucia's wails and bemoaning as the fire raged.

Finally, she fell to the ground and covered her two ears as she sobbed at the agony Lucia was feeling to pass through a cruel fate.

Lucinda couldn't believe Lucia was killed in such a horrible manner, which explained Anya's anger, who would always avenge her own.

Lucia was killed in such a horrible manner because she was mistaken to be the king's murderer. Despite her pleas of innocence, the people still killed her and to think that this was the same city she protected with all her life, the same people she healed, not to mention her countless goodness to them.

How they thought she could stoop so low to kill a mere human, the same humans she had protected all her life, was something incredible. She was burned to death. It was years already, but Anya could still hear her cry. She could still see how Lucia struggled to live. Lucia submitted herself to die so that her parents could live, but the people did not spare her parents too.

They had her parents killed and had their carcass fed to the birds of the air.

This was the act of wickedness that got Anya infuriated, and she came for vendetta. As the panorama of what happened played again in Anya's memory, she screamed as the bushes felt the gravity of her howls, which startled Lucinda.

"Lucia said she had forgiven them," Lucinda replied.

"But Anya never forgives. Anya believes in revenge. The city you wanted to save so badly killed you before, yet your heart is filled with mercy and compassion." Anya replied.

"Yes, besides feeling for them, I also feel for my grandparents, which could be hurt by you someday," Lucinda replied.

"That's true, but I will never kill them. I can only hurt them, as the killing has already stopped since the queen has welcomed me." Anya replied.

"How am I sure you won't hurt any more souls? They might have wronged me years back, but the old me forgave them even before my death. So, Anya, why can't you forgive? Please forgive and go back to the world which you came from." Lucinda replied.

"I can't!" Anya bellowed.

"But why? Why can't you? My grandparents are living in constant fear; the people too. Everyone is in fear, and to think that I brought this upon all of them and..."

"You didn't. They bought it upon themselves. They killed you even when you pleaded your innocence. How could they kill the soul that gave them everything? How could they betray her?" Anya screamed.

"I have forgiven them. Let peace reign. I don't want to cause chaos. Let this place be peaceful. Anya, my grandparents sleep with one eye closed and one eye open. You might not kill them, but you will hurt them someday.

I'm tired of people living in fear. I'm tired of hearing the cries of the people calling on me for help. Please, Anya, I'm begging you from the innermost of my being.

Let this go. Even if you can't forget, please forgive. I beg you as the daughter of the moon. Listen to me, Anya. Please." Lucinda said as she knelt and bowed her head.

"How could you?" Anya shouted.

Anya couldn't believe that Lucinda was ever going to kneel and bow before her. Now there was no way she was going to hurt anyone again. That act of Lucinda's humility has hindered her. Anya knew that once the queen bowed to her, whatever she needed must be granted.

"How could you, Lucinda? These people murdered you years ago. Why have you stopped me from hurting them? Why? I only wanted them to have a taste of what you went through in their hands. I haven't had the chance to grace the human world after Lucia's death, and now that I have the chance, my only aim is to kill as many as I can before I go. Why do you have to kneel and bow before me? Why Lucinda? Why did you have to do this?

Well, keep your powers hidden from the human eyes; otherwise, they might be forced to kill you again, labeling you a witch or a sorcerer or whatever they may fancy." Anya said as she howled so loud.

I just want to have my peace," Lucinda replied as she got up from the ground.

"We waited for you this long, and now you are here. You have stopped me from feeding the blood of these humans to the earth, although you're the earth goddess. You're just so compassionate." Anya howled as she raced off.

Lucinda kept looking at the three wolves before they went out of her sight. She sighed as she sat on the ground, wondering whether Anya would ever forget and forgive what the city people did to her years back.

AS SOON AS ANYA
DISAPPEARED

As soon as Anya disappeared, Lucinda stood up from the ground and headed back home, with too many thoughts raging in her infantile mind. So, she was the fourth goddess which summed up everything. They had waited patiently for her to become older before things would be revealed to her. But they should have waited until it was at least twenty before unleashing all these to me. So, she was still thinking as she walked home dejectedly, though happy with herself for at least being able to stop Anya.

When she got home, she went towards the backyard and stealthily entered inside through the backdoor. She locked the door behind her and went straight for her room. She knew she had just three hours to sleep. She lay on her bed, covering herself before she drifted off to sleep.

****

She saw herself taking a stroll somewhere unfamiliar when someone tapped her as she turned swiftly to see who it was. She was stunned to see a lady standing before her, with her skin glistening like the sun.

"Who is this?" Lucinda murmured, half audibly, impossible for the lady to hear, but she heard her.

"I'm such different things to different people. Perhaps you can choose a name for me." The lady replied.

"Your skin glistens like that of gems. Can I call you Sun?" Lucinda replied.

"I like the name." The lady replied, smiling.

"Who are you; I mean, what are you?" Lucinda asked.

"I'm Sun, just like you named me." She replied.

"No, not your name. I mean to know who are you and how can I help you?" Lucinda asked.

"You can't help me; rather, I'm here to help you. You seek answers. Mia, the river goddess, couldn't answer; Berta, the wind goddess, couldn't answer, and Tara, the Fire Goddess, couldn't answer. You are searching for answers, and I'm here to give them to you." Sun replied.

"Yes, I am. You're right. First, how can I send Anya back to the world she came from? Souls may still be lost if she keeps staying here." Lucinda asked.

"If Anya stops destroying humans, will you let her stay?" Sun asked.

"Yes, I will, but that's not possible; she is a deadly beast," Lucinda replied.

"That's the side you saw first, beside you have already welcomed her, and even knelt and bowed to her so that she won't hurt a single soul anymore," Sun replied.

"Even at that, how do I send her back?" Lucinda asked.

"You want Anya to leave so soon when you haven't even gotten to know her? Anya will leave when you don't expect it. It will come as a surprise to you. Anya was sent for a reason, not just to avenge your death. In the future, you would be glad you got to know her more." Sun replied

"So, I can't send her back?" Lucinda asked.

"I don't even know why you're so obsessed with sending her back. Well,

Anya can never leave; you can't send her back. You can only tame her." Sun replied.

"How do I tame her if I can't send her back?" Lucinda replied.

"That you have already done. You tamed Anya the minute you welcomed, knelt, and bowed before her. Henceforth, she will only take instructions from you. You're the queen, and she is your subject. I'm glad you listened to your father's voice instead of your mom's. Don't let fear win. I'm so happy you didn't give room for fear." Sun replied.

"You know so much about me already, and you know about my parents too?" Lucinda asked.

"Everyone knows the people who gave birth to the supreme queen, the daughter of the moon and the stars," Sun replied and came closer to Lucinda.

"What do you want to do?" Lucinda asked.

"I'm sending you back to your world. Our discussion here is ended." Sun replied.

"But I'm not through with my questions." Lucinda protested.

"You have always wanted to send Anya back, but that's not possible. So, the next question you wish to ask now is how to drop the crown on your head, that you don't want to be the queen anymore. Am I right?" Sun asked.

"Yes, you're right. I'm not interested in any of these. I just want to be free and live like the normal young girl that I am." Lucinda replied.

"That's not possible! You can't be what you are not or not be what you are. You have always been the queen, even before the birth of your mom, Anna. So don't blame your mother for the wish she made. It has always been your fate." Sun replied as she touched Lucinda on her forehead.

Lucinda opened her eyes slowly, only to realize she had been dreaming. She sat up straight and looked at herself in the mirror.

It has never been Mom's fault. I had always been destined to be a queen. So, Lucinda thought as she stood up slowly and made for her window to open it. It was already morning. The sunrays were already streaming in upon earth. After opening the windows, she went back to her back and took her clothes out as she quickly rushed into the bathroom to have her bath and brushed her teeth, after which she wore her clothes and walked into the sitting room.

"Good morning, Granny," Lucinda said to Maya, who was busy slicing the onions.

"Good morning, my dear. You woke up late. I came to your room to check on you only to discover you were asleep, and I didn't want to disturb you, so I allowed sleep on." Maya replied.

"Oh, good of you, Grandma. What are you making breakfast?" Lucinda asked.

"It's a surprise, and guess what, no single soul was lost last night. So, guess the beasts didn't visit again, after all. I think they are gone for good." Maya replied.

,

"They are not gone; they are around," Lucinda replied.

"How do you mean they are still around? Explain better." Maya replied.

"That they didn't hurt anyone last night does not mean they are gone. They they live with us now. That they are calm now is because of one reason. They will never leave. This is now their new home." Lucinda replied.

"Is there anything you're not telling me?" Maya asked, eyeing Lucinda.

"I just told you everything you need to know. They are not gone; they are still around, and they are never leaving until they decide to do so." Lucinda replied.

"Lucinda!" Maya called.

"Ask no more questions, Granny, I'm begging you," Lucinda replied as she stood up and walked to the kitchen to get drinking water for herself.

The day went well as Lucinda eagerly waited for nightfall. She wanted to see Anya. Eventually, it was night. So, Lucinda kept the back door unlocked, and when she was sure her grandparents were asleep, she crept out of the house, heading to where she had met with Anya the previous night, getting there just a few minutes before midnight.

"I hope you haven't been waiting for long, my queen?" It was Anya. Lucinda turned back to see Anya. There she was, with eyes glistening.

"Not too long as I needed my grandparents to be asleep before I could come out," Lucinda replied.

"But how come you're now one? I thought you're three in one?" Lucinda asked.

"In my body, the other two comes out only when the need arises. They can hear me; they can speak through me.

I'm the enchanted wolf of the moon and the stars. Some see me as the deadliest beast because I'm three in one; while I show no mercy when I torment, but fate has it that the only one who I can ever obey is you.

That was why on the day you were born; your people heard howls of wolves. It was me paying my respect." Anya replied.

Lucinda heaved a sigh of relief on hearing the last words before uttering: "You won't hurt anyone ever again, please. I wouldn't want to be the reason for people's pains." Lucinda pleaded.

"As you wish, Your Majesty," Anya replied as she slowly transformed into a lady in her late twenties. Lucinda was shocked at sighting that. She couldn't believe her eyes. She blinked a million times under a second.

"How did you do that?" She finally found her voice to ask.

"I'm Anya, an enchanted wolf. I can transform to anything I wish, and that's what happens when you are blessed with powers; that's why they call me the deadliest." She replied as she smiled.

"In that case, guess I will come here every night to see you. Hope I'll always see you?" Lucinda asked.

"Of course, you will," Anya replied as she stretched forth her hand and handed a necklace to Lucinda.

"What will I do with this?" Lucinda asked.

"It has always been yours. You need this to activate the powers which you possess. Lucinda, you are royalty, though you are yet to realize that." Anya remarked.

"I accept who I am. It won't lead anywhere if I keep blaming Mom or rejecting it. I accept, and I agree that this girl here called Lucinda is the daughter of the moon and the stars." Lucinda said, sighing at the same time.

And soon, there was the flash of lightning followed by the rumbling of thunder. Lucinda cowered and held onto Anya tightly as she was frightened, but Anya remained calm.

"Seems you're scared of the lightning? No need for that. It was just a sign that the world beyond has heard you. Now, look up." Anya said as Lucinda slowly looked up.

"The sky was filled with stars, and it looked so beautiful." Anya pointed at the stars and smiled.

"You are blessed with the greatest power of them all; the power to heal and the power to hurt anyone with just your pair of eyes," Anya replied.

"How can I hurt someone just by merely looking at them?" Lucinda asked.

"Maybe there is only one way to find out. Look that cobra slithering over there," Anya pointed at a snake coming towards them.

Lucinda stood up quickly and held onto Anya as she shouted, "Kill the snake."

Anya kept quiet as she watched Lucinda, a look that reminded her of what she just told her a second ago. Lucinda caught the prompt and looked at the snake. Lucinda turned to balls of fire on closing and opening them, and as she looked at the snake, it just dried up instantly, dead.

"What just happened to me?" Lucinda, shocked, asked as soon as she got hold of herself.

"You just killed the snake. Be quick to call yourself back to reality, so you don't hurt someone else." Anya told her.

"Can you help me with the necklace?" Lucinda asked.

"Sure," Anya said as Lucinda positioned herself while Anya helped her with the necklace.

"You look pretty." Anya complimented.

"Thank you," Lucinda replied, smiling.

"Anya, I have a question troubling my mind. I met this lady who told me a time would come when choosing between my parents and saving humanity. I didn't understand what she meant, and I still don't understand, but it still troubles my mind. I want answers, please."

"Yes, what she said is true. It was the Wind Goddess who told you that. Berta was right. Indeed, the time comes when you have to choose, but no one knows what is going to happen." Anya replied.

"My parents are dead, and I can only hear their voice. How do I have to choose between them and saving humanity? How? I don't understand." Lucinda asked.

"I do not know my queen, but a queen faces myriads of trials and tribulations but what makes her a real queen is how she handles the situation.

You already passed the first trial, remaining the second, and no one knows what that will be. So, get yourself ready. I'm glad you listened to your father's voice when he urged you not to give in to fear.

Do not allow fear winning." Anya said, standing up.

"Where are you going," Lucinda asked.

"It's already 3 am, and you need to go home, Lucinda," Anya replied.

"Wow! I didn't know how time flies. Aren't you leaving so soon?" Lucinda replied.

"Well, neither here nor there. I need you to sleep. I wouldn't want to keep you awake, and when I leave, I want you to hold the necklace and think of your room. Just do that." Anya replied as she squatted and slowly transformed into a wolf. She looked at Lucinda one more time before she raced into the bushes, disappearing.

Lucinda waved at her as she slowly closed her eyes, touching the necklace, and then thought of her room. On opening her eyes, she saw herself standing right inside her room.

It then dawned on Lucinda that what she had on her neck was not an ordinary necklace. With this, Lucinda knew she could teleport anywhere. It was an exciting feeling.

Lucinda walked to her mirror to admire her new necklace, with a unique sense of exhilaration. However, she was feeling sleepy already. She turned to her bed and switched her mind to all that happened that night.

She was awoken in the morning by the assuring hands of Maya on her shoulders as she still lay on the bed. On getting up, she saw her grandmother sitting close to her on the bed.

"Good morning, Grandma." Lucinda greeted.

"Good morning? It's afternoon, baby girl! Maya replied.

"What? Are you serious? I didn't know." Lucinda said sitting up, as she stretched her dress.

"You awake all the night, right?" Maya asked, eyeing her suspiciously.

"Yes, I was, but that's not an issue. I had something to deal with it, and I had already sorted it out." Lucinda replied.

"Who gave you that necklace on your neck?" Maya asked, touching the pendant, which had the shape of the moon surrounded by stars.

"Oh, it's a gift," Lucinda replied.

"From who? I didn't see this on your neck throughout yesterday until when you retired to your room, and how come you slept and woke up with it? What are you not telling me, Lucinda?" Maya asked, still not satisfied with Lucinda's answer.

"There is nothing to know, Grandma. It's a gift from my parents. I refused to show it to anyone, and it has been with me ever since they died. So, I just felt like wearing it yesterday before I went to bed." Lucinda lied, an unavoidable lie.

"You're lying to me," Maya remarked.

"Why would I lie to you?" Lucinda asked, standing up.

"I didn't ask you a question. I know you lied because this is real gold with diamond stones encrusted on the pendant. How did Anna and Phil get such money to buy such an expensive necklace? This necklace sure costs a fortune." Maya replied.

"Maybe if they were alive, you would have asked them how they got the money to buy the necklace." Lucinda insisted as she brought out the clothes she was going to wear. She left her grandmother sitting on the bed as she walked into the bathroom to have her bath.

Maya wouldn't want to wait for her to come out. She stood up and left the room to meet Greg to tell him about the necklace.

When Lucinda finished bathing, she wore her clothes and instinctively looked at the pendant one more time before leaving her room.

****

"I don't know how Lucinda came about the necklace she is wearing. That necklace is real gold and diamond, and it must have cost a fortune." Maya said.

"How sure are you?" Greg asked.

"I can't make up stories," Maya replied.

"Good afternoon, Grandpa," Lucinda greeted as she sat on the floor, and as soon Maya walked closer to her and pulled out the pendant from Lucinda's neck.

"Are you not seeing that this is real gold and diamond?" Maya said, throwing it at Greg. But Lucinda wouldn't have any of that. So instead, she retrieved the necklace from Greg's hand and placed it inside her clothes.

"Lucinda, do you have any explanations on how you came about the necklace?" Greg asked.

"I already told Granny. It's from my parents. It has been with me all the while, only that I've been reluctant in wearing it." Lucinda replied.

"And how come we have never seen it? How come you've kept that away from us for so long? Besides, Anna and Phil are our children; there is no way to afford something as expensive as this. So, tell me, where did you get the necklace from?" Greg asked.

Lucinda kept mute as she ran her hands on her hair, as she thought of what more to say.

"Lucinda, talk." Maya threatened, widening her eyes.

"Grandpa, didn't you always say that though my parents had nothing, they still wanted to give me the entire world?" Lucinda asked.

"Yes, I said so. It's true." Greg concurred.

"You once told me the story behind my birth. I asked you if I'm the daughter of the moon and the stars, and you told me yes," Lucinda asked.

"Yes, I did," Greg replied, not sure of where Lucinda was driving to.

"What's the symbol on this pendant?" Lucinda asked.

"The moon surrounded by the stars." Greg and Maya replied in unison.

"Well, Mom and Dad might have nothing, but they will give me everything. They were ever willing to give me the world if possible.

That they didn't tell you about the necklace doesn't mean they didn't buy it. I already told you, and I'm repeating it, it's from them. I kept it away for years because I wanted to." Lucinda said as she stood up; and walked into the kitchen, being already famished.

"I don't believe her," Maya said.

"Same here, but she already said it is from her parents, and of course, there is nothing we can do about it. Her parents aren't here, so who are we going to ask?" Greg replied.

Maya sighed as she sat down abruptly on the sofa. Lucinda walked out of the kitchen carrying a plate of food and went straight to her room. Once inside, Lucinda sat down as she gently ate her food in silence.

On coming out of her room, Lucinda informed her grandparents that she wanted to take a stroll on the street. Lucinda then left the house and started walking down the road.

As she walked about, a little girl suddenly from nowhere hit her, falling. She bent down to help the girl stand on her feet again.

"What's your name?" Lucinda asked.

"My name is Amber." The little girl replied.

"Where are your parents? You shouldn't be all alone on the street." Lucinda said, looking around as she held tightly on the girl.

"Thank you very much," Amber said, smiling.

"And why are you thanking me?" Lucinda asked.

"For taming Anya, and don't worry about sending her back as she will be of great use to you later. Trust me. You look beautiful, daughter of the moon and the stars." Amber replied as she smiled, flashing her excellent dentition as Lucinda stepped back and mopped at her in awe.

Shortly after, an aged woman appeared and held onto Amber.

"I'm so sorry; she is my granddaughter. I didn't know when she ran off. Hope she wasn't saying silly kinds of stuff to you?" The aged woman asked.

"No, not all," Lucinda replied.

"I finally met the daughter of the moon and the stars. It's such an honor." Amber said excitedly as they still stood before Lucinda.

"You better keep quiet. Someone would never believe you're just six, yet you speak way past your age. I'm so sorry," the aged woman apologized before she left with Amber.

Lucinda smiled as she turned and walked back home. She knew the little girl wasn't an ordinary girl. Amber was a seer, and with time, Amber would get to realize the power she possessed. When Lucinda got home, she walked straight to her room, and lying on the bed; she slept off. She needed to sleep since she was going out to meet with Anya later in the night.

She later woke up late in the evening and went straight to the kitchen to pick up her dinner, after which she went back to her room and locked her door behind her.

"Are you going anywhere?" Her mom's voice spoke.

"Yes, Mom. I'm going to meet with Anya." Lucinda replied.

"You can't go; Anya might hurt you one day." She pleaded.

"Anya can't hurt me. I'm her queen. Have you ever heard a subject hurting the one who wears the crown? I possess powers greater than anyone else, including her. She can't hurt me. Not possible anymore." Lucinda replied.

"Who are you? You have changed." She remarked.

"I didn't change, Mother. Remember when you said I'm the daughter of the moon and the stars? You wanted me to be queen over all others. Well, I am now what you wished me to be." Lucinda replied.

"Please be safe. I might be dead, but I can't bear it to watch anything happen to my only child." Anna replied.

"Alright, Mom. I'll be safe. My greetings to Dad." Lucinda replied.

Lucinda lay on her bed as she waited for some minutes before midnight. By then, her grandparents must be fully asleep. Once it was time for her to leave, she stood up and closed her eyes. Then, thinking of their meeting place and touching her necklace, she instantly teleported to the location.

She sat on the floor as she waited gently for midnight when Anya would appear. Instead, she started hearing the howl of wolves. Not long after, Lucinda felt someone tap her shoulder and turned to see it was Anya. She watched her as she changed into a beautiful young lady.

"Amber: you will have to find her because you need her in this journey," Anya said as soon as she completed her transformation while sitting down next to Lucinda.

"You know her? She is just six, as her granny said. But how did you get to know about her?" Lucinda replied.

"My name is Anya, an enchanted wolf, the three in one beast. I know things you don't know in your present phase as a mortal. Amber is a seer.

Remember she said it was an honor to meet you. But if I told you that the little girl you saw today is just an old woman in the body of a child? Amber knows more than you do.

In her past life, she waited and prayed to see you, but she didn't; and now that she saw you for the first time in her existence, she was excited beyond words." Anya replied.

"How do I find her then? How do I go about looking for her? It's going to be very difficult, and how do I even need her on this journey? Everyone keeps talking about the journey. What journey is that?" Lucinda asked, a little furious.

"With time, you will know. But the truth is you have to find Amber. She sees things that the human eyes can't see. Amber is the key you would need in the future." Anya replied.

"I will try to find her. Hopefully, I will find her in less than a week." Lucinda replied.

"I never thought the goodbye would happen soon," Anya said, looking around.

"What do you mean?" Lucinda asked.

"Again, with time, you will understand. As for the necklace, don't worry, your grandparents won't question you about it anymore. Stay safe and strong, and never let fear win over you. Always have faith in yourself that you're always capable.

The road will be filled with temptation, tribulations but worry not because I have always seen you as a winner. You will emerge victoriously. Try to keep your powers away from human eyes." Anya said.

"Why are you telling me all these? What's the problem? Is there anything that is going to happen that I'm not aware of? Please let me know; don't keep me in suspense. Let me know so I can know how to brace myself up for it." Lucinda said.

"I have to go now, and you have to go home too," Anya said as she swiftly turned into a wolf. Then, touching her paws on Lucinda's hand, she shifted backward, bowing down to Lucinda, after which she disappeared into the bush.

With tears in her eyes, Lucinda touched her necklace, and immediately she was home. She knew something was off, and she was determined to find out from Anya what the problem was by tomorrow.

In the morning, Lucinda woke up and went about with her duties. She ate her breakfast and retired back to her bedroom without talking to anyone. She was eager for the night to come so she could meet Anya.

As usual, Lucinda appeared at the bush path she always met with Anya before midnight, but when it struck midnight, she heard no howl. She waited patiently, but Anya never came, and when it was almost daybreak,

Lucinda had to return home with her heart filled with pain and anger. Where did Anya go? She wondered.

Greg and Maya noticed Lucinda's mood throughout that day and kept asking what was wrong, but she kept it to herself. She just didn't want to talk about it because she knew they wouldn't understand.

She just wanted Anya; she wanted to see her face again. She needed her so badly. Why would she come into her life and leave so soon, without warning?

As she paced about her room, tensed an idea came to her to go back to their meeting place.

She then walked into the stable and took out the white horse. She mounted and raced off to the bush path where she usually met with Anya. When she got there, she came down and tied the horse to a tree.

"Anya!!! Where are you?" Lucinda shouted.

She called three more times, but all she received in return was a deafening silence.

She went deeper into the bush, hoping to see Anya, but nothing was found. Finally, she came out with tears in her eyes, and untying the horse, she mounted it and rode back home, dejected.

When she got home, she took the horse inside and locked the stable as she went into the house.

"Lucinda, you're back; come and have lunch. You have had nothing to eat since morning." Maya said as soon as she sighted Lucinda.

"I'm not hungry, Grandma," Lucinda replied.

"Why? You left this morning having nothing to eat, and now you're saying you're not hungry? What's the problem? You have been moody since morning. Maya has been asking what the problem is, yet you kept mute." Greg chipped in.

I'm not hungry. I will be in my room and don't bother checking up on me. I'm fine." Lucinda said as she walked out when Maya called her back.

"You're not fine. Look at your eyes. They are red. You have been crying. What's the problem, girl?" Maya asked.

"I said I'm fine," Lucinda shouted as she ran into her room and banged the door. She made sure she locked the door from inside to stop her grandparents from coming inside. She just wanted to be alone.

After that day, on the following nights, Lucinda would make sure she went to the bush path to wait for Anya, but she never showed up, and it felt like Lucinda was slowly losing herself.

She had formed this bond with Anya in a short time that she couldn't believe she was gone.

Every day Lucinda would lock herself in the room thinking about Anya. She would remember everything that happened between them within the past few days that they were together.

Time was going fast, and it was already four months since Anya left Lucinda, but that didn't stop Lucinda from going out to wait for her. She had this hope of meeting her again.

As Lucinda lay down on her bed on a particular evening, she felt a decisive breeze blow. A heavy downpour started within a few minutes, which made her get up and walked closer to the window to inhale the husky smell of the saturated soil.

"What is bothering you, my child? You have been like this for the past four months now, with no sign of it abetting. So, what is the problem?" Her mom's voice chimed through.

"Mom, Anya is gone. It's four months now, and Anya is yet to return. What's keeping her? Have they killed her? I can't even communicate through dreams anymore. It's been nothing since I saw her last. It seemed as if everything went with Anya." Lucinda replied, crying.

"But you wanted her to go. Why are you bothered about her now?" She asked.

"Mom, I wanted her to leave then but not now. After I got to find out who the real Anya is, I fell in love with her. She has a sweet soul, and there is a reason for the people she killed. I simply miss her company. These past four months have never been the same without her." Lucinda replied.

"So, what are you going to do?" The voice asked.

"Nothing. I don't know how to even communicate with Anya. I don't know what to do. The least I can do is just to go out there every night to wait for her believing that someday she is going to come back." Lucinda replied.

"Lucinda, Anya might never come back. You just have to accept it and live your life." Anna said.

"That's the problem. Why does life bring people to me, and just when I have formed a bond with them, life takes them away? Why is that so? Why is my own life designed that way? Why do I always have to lose people I love along the way?

I'm tired of it. First, they took you and Dad away from me when I was just ten, and now, they have taken Anya away. Who knows who is next, Grandpa or even Grandma? I'm tired of everything." Lucinda said as she wiped the tears off her eyes.

"You miss Anya. I hope she comes back, and if she doesn't, I hope this rain washes away the pain in your heart." Anna consoled.

****

It was just a matter of time before Anya comes back. How long will Lucinda be able to cope with the absence of her parents' voices and the disappearance of Anya?

◆ ◆ ◆

ABOUT THE AUTHOR

Dennis W.C. Wong was born at Kapiolani Hospital in Honolulu, Oahu, in the territory of Hawaii in 1951.

He found out from a lady in a gift shop that the hospital had to move its Labor and Delivery Department into the basement after the attack on Pearl Harbor, then moved again to the third floor. This was to ensure the safety of the pregnant mothers and their babies, of which he and his mother Katherine were part of.